ALL THAT GLITTERS

A GREAT WESTERN DETECTIVE LEAGUE CASE

ALL THAT GLITTERS

PAUL COLT

FIVE STAR
A part of Gale, Cengage Learning

GALE
CENGAGE Learning·

Farmington Hills, Mich • San Francisco • New York • Waterville, Maine
Meriden, Conn • Mason, Ohio • Chicago

GALE
CENGAGE Learning®

LIBRARY OF CONGRESS CATALOGING-IN-PUBLICATION DATA

Names: Colt, Paul, author.
Title: All that glitters : a Great Western Detective League case/ Paul Colt. Description: First edition. I Farmington Hills, Mich.: Five Star, a part of
Gale, Cengage Learning, [2019]
Identifiers: LCCN 20.18025274 (print) I LCCN 2018027768 (ebook) I ISBN 9781432849573 (ebook) I ISBN 9781432849566 (ebook) | ISBN 9781432849559 (hardcover)
Subjects: I GSAFD: Mystery fiction. I Western stories.
Classification: LCC PS3603.04673 (ebook) I LCC PS3603.04673 A79 2019 (print) I DDC 813/—dc23
LC record available at https://lccn.loc.gov/2018025274

First Edition. First Printing: January 2019
Find us on Facebook—https://www.facebook.com/FiveStarCengage
Visit our website—http://www.gale.cengage.com/fivestar/
Contact Five Star Publishing at FiveStar©cengage.com

Printed in Mexico
1 2 3 4 5 6 7 23 22 21 20 19

ALL THAT GLITTERS

PROLOGUE

China Town
San Francisco
February 1, 1878

A cool winter breeze pushed a light veil of fog off the bay, flavored with a hint of salt tang. Inclement elements did little to dampen the festival unfolding below. Strings of brightly colored paper lanterns lit narrow warren-ways filled with gaily clad revelers. Cymbals clashed atop a rhythmic cadence of heavy drums. A giant green dragon, its silken scales and fiery eyes alight, danced through the streets followed by a merry, boisterous throng of revelers.

Two blocks east on a deserted section of Montgomery, near the Embarcadero, a rundown brick building stood dark and silent in the middle of the block beside its neighbors, distinguished only by a sign, lettered in chipped gold leaf, reading, *International Imports*. Inside, a dark hulk crouched in a back corner. Faint light from an upper window provided all the illumination the man needed, conducting his business more by feel than sight. Metal on metal ground softly as a sharp bit painstakingly bore its way into the gray steel door just above the silvery locking mechanism. Beads of perspiration stood out on a shining, black, bald pate, bent to the task. At last the bit broke through.

The dark figure straightened, nearly as tall as the silhouette of the safe, though still on his knees. He replaced the drill in a case at his side and withdrew a small box. He held it firm out of abiding respect for its contents. Thick fingers, seemingly ill-suited to so delicate a purpose, unfastened the tiny hasp. The box opened to a tiny vial, resting on a velvet cushion. He lifted the vial, and crystal liquid shimmered in dark light, precisely measured to the task of the old Chubb Lilly. He felt the face of the door, found his hole, and inserted the vial gently in its place. He covered the opening with a revolver cap and a bit of fuse and sealed it all with softened beeswax. He let out a satisfied breath. He had only to wait for the climactic moment.

He gathered his case and made his way to the far corner of the room, safely behind the customer counter. He left the case and returned to wait beside the safe.

Up the street in Chinatown the celebration built to a raucous crescendo of anticipation. It began slowly. A muffled thump. The sky filled with glorious colored blossoms accompanied by hushed responses from the crowd. More thumps birthed bright bursts in the sky, gasps of hurrah punctuated by trailing claps of powder boom.

Over on Montgomery, the intruder listened. Bright colored flashes lit the darkness; their explosive concussions rattled the windows. The expected barrage would follow on cue, drawing the festivities to a close. The moment had arrived. Lucifer flared sulphur smoke. Fuse hissed to light. The dark figure dashed across the darkened office, hopping the counter with a grace belied by his bulk. He covered his ears as his firework burst among the crescendo bursting above.

Smoke stung his eyes. No time to waste. He grabbed his case, choking smoke as he crossed the office to the blown door. He reached inside. Felt sacks, first one, then two, now three. He placed the first two in his case. The third he could not resist. His stinging eyes watered. Still he opened the sack and poured some of its contents into his hand. Even in soft light, they glittered through his tears—diamonds, a fortune in diamonds.

He returned them to the sack and placed it in his case. He closed the case and made his way to the shop rear door. The alley beyond remained dark and deserted. He stepped outside, filled his lungs with clean air. He closed the shop door and casually strolled down the alley and up the hill toward the sounds of New Year merriment.

CHAPTER ONE

Denver

Shady Grove Rest Home and Convalescent Center

1909

I trudged up the hill to my regular appointment on a sunny spring Saturday morning, a bulge in one coat pocket and a brown wrapped package under my arm. By way of introduction for those whom I may not have met, my name is Robert Brentwood. I beg indulgence of those who may be familiar with this part of the story, but I should explain for the benefit of those new to these adventures. I am employed as a reporter for the *Denver Tribune*, though in this venture I've come to compile the stories of the Great Western Detective League. The idea for this project first occurred to me when I stumbled on reports of this association of law enforcement professionals in the *Tribune* archives. Imagine my surprise when I discovered, quite by accident, the mastermind behind this storied network of crime fighters still alive and comfortably ensconced at the Shady Grove Rest Home and Convalescent Center. My nascent writing career seemed foreordained by the discovery.

As things have come to pass, the Colonel, David J. Crook (US Army Ret.), agreed to assist me in my ambition in return for . . . modest compensation, as we shall presently see. In return we've completed two stories, dramatizing the extraordinary exploits of the Colonel's legendary organization. Well, perhaps not yet legendary; it shall certainly be so before we are finished. The Colonel and I have struck up something of a remarkable relationship over his telling of these tales. I shall leave you to formulate your own impression of the Colonel as this story unfolds.

I have come to regard him with admiration and affection, though, I must admit, he can be vexing at times. I find myself indebted to him not only for his stories, but also for an amazing possibility come into my life by his intervention. The Colonel took it upon himself to introduce me to his attendant, Miss Penny O'Malley. He did so out of the irascible conviction he might not live long enough to see me speak for myself. That is quintessentially the Colonel. He is an incorrigible tease who feels perfectly permitted to barge into any private affair without regard to social convention or the least consideration for proper restraint. He did, of course, gain the desired result. My relationship with Penny has grown to the point where, given the contents of the package under my arm, I've come to think of a more permanent state to our relationship. My relationship with Penny that is.

On this particular Saturday, the nurse stationed in a spacious, pleasant reception hall greeted me with her usual conspiratorial smile.

"She is in the refectory. He is on the veranda, I believe. Take your choice."

I smiled. "I'm here to see the Colonel."

She nodded a condescending "of course" toward the veranda. Much as we have endeavored to keep our romance private, clearly we have failed. The Colonel tells me I have only my lovely Penny to thank for that, romance being a favored topic among the gentle sex. If he is right, I fear there is much more here I've yet to understand.

I found him in his usual place, comfortably seated in his wheeled chair at the far end of a sun-splashed veranda looking

up to the ragged peaks of the front-range. The Colonel generally sat his chair ramrod straight with an air that denied the rav-
ages of his eighty years. Today I noted he slumped a bit, perhaps
having caught him in the act of a nap. Still he preferred the
fresh mountain air of a crisp spring day to the stuffy over-warm
interior maintained for Shady Grove residents. The only concession he permitted to the cool air—a blanket wrapped around
his legs. His thick white hair and bushy mutton chops had yel-
lowed a bit in these past few years, though his watery blue eyes
still managed to retain the calm, cool measure of his younger
years. He possessed a keen, intuitive wit that distinguished his
career as a master investigator and the driving force behind the
storied Great Western Detective League. The daring deeds of
that distinguished organization and the countless adventures
recorded in their case files were etched like a map in the
wrinkled features of the man who recalled them all.

I drew up a chair and sat beside him. His breathing was
regular deep in his chest. His head bobbed. He blinked. Looked
up to the peaks and sensed my presence.

"Robert, is that you?"

"It is, sir."

"You're late."

Of course I wasn't.

He glanced over my shoulder. Satisfied we were alone, he
fumbled under his lap robe and produced an empty whiskey
bottle. I removed a full bottle from the bulge in my coat pocket
and exchanged it for the empty. The matter of his compensation
for the week concluded, he hid it in his lap robe. I sometimes
wondered if the sole purpose the robe served was the hiding of
his contraband whiskey, which I supplied at no small risk to my
romantic situation. Strong spirits are strictly forbidden at Shady
Grove and chief enforcer of the Colonel's conformance to rules
and schedules, none other than my beloved Penny.

"I've something else for you today."

He bunched his moustache under the wrinkled bridge of his nose, curious. "Oh, what might that be?"

I handed him the brown wrapped bundle.

He turned it over as if uncertain.

"Go ahead, open it."

He did so, peeling back the butcher paper to reveal a book. He turned to the spine.

"Wanted: Sam Bass, A Great Western Detective League Case."

He lifted a moistened eye to me.

"You did it, Robert. Well done, son."

He'd never called me son before. I must admit, it caught in my throat. A new bit of pride to add to that already accomplished.

"I couldn't have done it without you, Colonel."

"Of course you couldn't, and never forget your indebtedness. Still, I'm damn proud of you. What about our Bogus Bondsman?"

"My publisher is considering it. I hope to hear something soon."

He coughed. "I suppose that means we shall need another story then."

"Indeed. Have you given any thought to one?"

"Not really. Let's see . . ."

"While you think, might I impose on you for a bit of advice?" I really hadn't planned to bring this up with him. The Colonel had a way of running away with such matters, though I did respect his experience, and I suspect his calling me "son" whetted my appetite for fatherly advice.

"Advice, of course. Old men aren't good for much more. We give it freely, which assures the value you give it."

"I've spoken to a jeweler in regard to the purchase of a ring."

He favored me with an expression I regret to say I am at a

loss to describe.

"A ring. Of the nuptial variety?"

I'm quite sure I flushed. "Yes."

"It's a big step."

"I know."

"But then again, not so big for a prosperous young author."

"Prosperous may be getting ahead of ourselves, though I did receive a modest advance on sales of the book."

"What sort of ring are you interested in that requires the advice of an old man?"

"Tradition of course is a simple gold or silver band. The jeweler suggests the latest fashion is a band with a stone."

"A stone?"

"Yes, a diamond seems to be preferred."

"Sounds expensive. You said this advance was modest."

"The jeweler calls it an investment."

"An investment . . . hmm. Yes, I suppose he would see it that way. I'm not sure what to tell you of that, Robert. It strikes me you'd be equally wed with or without a stone. I suspect you will have to let your heart decide the right of that course. It does help with one matter, though."

"What's that?"

"Our next story. As the saying goes, 'All that glitters isn't gold.' We got quite an education on the fine points of that old bromide back in seventy-eight."

I drew out my notebook.

CHAPTER TWO

Denver

February 14, 1878

It started like many another winter day in Denver. Overnight snow thawing to wet puddles by midday, belying impassible mountain passes north and west of town. A stylish gentleman in an English tweed overcoat presented himself at the office with a request to see me. I directed he be shown into my office. Lean and fit, his impeccably trimmed graying mustache and beard matched a gray suit and cravat. Bright-blue eyes contrasted with the understated palette of his attire. He presented a card along with an offered hand.

"Colonel Crook, Montegue Malthus, Claims Special Agent, Comprehensive Insurance Company."

I shook his hand. "Mr. Malthus, please, have a seat." He settled into a side chair, crossing polished boots at the ankle. "How might we be of service?"

"One of our clients has suffered a loss."

"Ah, a claim then. Am I to assume this claim," I glanced at his card, "is special?"

"We consider sixty thousand dollars in diamonds and assorted precious stones special indeed."

"I see. How then might we be of assistance?"

"Given the nature of the crime, local law enforcement has thrown up their hands beyond the limits of their jurisdiction. They recommended we bring the matter to your attention. They tell us your organization is able to reach across law enforcement jurisdictions."

"We do."

"May I ask how you manage that?"

"We are an association of law enforcement professionals, operating across the west. Investigations are coordinated out of this office by the distribution of information. Field work is led by our special agents, to borrow your term, augmented by local law enforcement officers who are members of the association. Our members share in the proceeds of retainers and rewards for recoveries associated with our cases. This assures full co-operation and exchange of the best available information."

"I see. In this matter I am authorized to offer a reward of fifteen thousand dollars for the recovery of the stolen merchandise. Would such an amount be sufficient to engage the services of your association?"

"Most certainly."

"Splendid. Then how shall we proceed?"

"The client's name?"

"International Imports."

"Address?"

"Montgomery Street, San Francisco."

"When did the loss occur?"

"The third of this month."

"Eleven days ago."

"To be precise."

"I shall dispatch two of my best investigators to the scene forthwith." I held up his card. "May I reach you at this address when we have something to report?"

"Of course."

"Very well then."

Malthus departed by waiting carriage. I summoned Cane to my office. He folded himself into one of my side chairs.

"What was that all about?" he said, nodding his head in the direction of my departed guest.

"Sixty thousand dollars in diamonds and assorted precious stones." I had his attention.

I'd admired Briscoe Cane's work for some time before I succeeded in engaging him to the firm. He wore a lean, weather-lined expression that might have been stitched out of old saddle leather, with hawk-like features punctuated by cold, gray eyes that seemed animated by some inner light. Barbered hair and drooping moustache, prematurely gray, along with a lean and angular, awkward appearing hickory hard frame aged him. For the object of one of his pursuits, misestimating his appearance might prove fatal.

Cane possessed cat like quickness in the use of a veritable arsenal of weaponry he concealed under a black frock coat. He favored a pair of fine, balanced bone-handled blades sheathed behind his .44 holster rig and in his left boot. He could draw and throw with either hand fast enough to silently defeat another man's gun draw. He was equally fast with the Colt and a .41 caliber Forehand & Wadsworth "Bull Dog" rigged for cross draw at his back. Some thought the spur trigger back-up gun the weapon of choice for a whore. Perhaps so, but then those who misestimated Cane seldom did so for long. He was expert with a Henry rifle that could pluck out an eye at a thousand paces. When a situation dictated, he possessed the skills of a master craftsman in the use of explosives. But for the religious foundation afforded by his upbringing, he might have found a prosperous career as an assassin. The most intriguing aspects of Cane, however, were his instincts. He saw things. He sensed things with an uncanny capacity for devious thinking. In pursuit, I swear he could track a fart in a snow storm.

I finished my report on the Malthus meeting.

"So I'm off to San Francisco."

"You and Longstreet. I say, where is Beau?"

"Went home to lunch with the widow."

"Of course. Track him down. Fill him in whilst he packs. Catch the next stage to Cheyenne . . ."

"And the first train to San Francisco."

He finished for me.

CHAPTER THREE

Beau Longstreet ambled up the tree-lined lane in fluid strides. One of those unseasonably warm, sunny days brightened midwinter along the front-range. Tall, muscular, and handsome, Longstreet's family roots ran deep in the old South. He came from the fringes of the more prominent Longstreet line best known for his cousin, the daring general who served under Robert E. Lee. Beau followed the family military tradition in service to the southern cause without the privilege of West Point education. He parlayed his family name into a junior officer's appointment and rose to the rank of captain before the cessation of hostilities. Humiliated in defeat, he drifted west, reaching St. Louis penniless. He signed on as a Pinkerton guard out of necessity and soon demonstrated a knack for protection. They'd done a good deal of defending in the later stages of the war. His experience as a field commander soon distinguished his performance for the Pinkerton agency. He gained greater responsibility in his assignments and, as the company followed the railroads and goldfields west, so also did Beau Longstreet.

A devil-may-care lady's man by nature, on a case he was circumspect, logical, and intuitive. He signed onto General Cook's detective association in Denver after encountering Cane in their pursuit of the notorious train robber Sam Bass. He soon impressed his new employer as a master investigator. Longstreet came in for the tough cases. He had a knack for the subtle clue, the overlooked fact, a cold trail, and the foibles of human nature.

He turned in at the gate to a stately, three-story, whitewashed Victorian situated in the center of a tree-lined block. It sat behind a wrought-iron fence, fronted by carefully tended gardens. He swung through the gate and climbed the steps to the broad front porch of the home where he maintained a room. He paused at the carved front door, bordered in frosted cut-glass windows with lace curtains.

Flowers would have added a perfect touch to this surprise had he thought of it. Then again, such a gesture was sure to invite speculation.

He knocked at the door. Presently footfalls sounded on the polished wood floor within. Silhouetted in lace, Maddie O'Rourke opened the door to quizzical surprise.

"What brings you home this time of day, and why knock? Lose your key?"

"Now there's a cheerful greeting if I ever heard one. I've merely come to offer the lady a bite of lunch lest she be forced to eat it alone. As to the knock, I didn't wish to alarm you."

The widow O'Rourke supported herself in a man's world operating a boarding house. A fine figure of a woman, she had wholesome good looks with waves of auburn hair tied up in a kerchief with an errant wisp escaped to one cheek. Girlish golden freckles splashed lightly across the bridge of an upturned pixie nose were the only flaw to a perfect porcelain complexion. She spoke the buttery brogue of her immigrant heritage with a merry laugh and deep-green eyes holding a mischievous twinkle. In a town starved for female companionship, Maddie O'Rourke stood apart. She had a stubborn independent steak that suited her temperament. The whole of her made a captivating challenge to Longstreet.

"Lunch, you say., I suppose that would be that hamper you carry."

"Hamper? I thought we might stroll downtown."

"And me in my work clothes for the chores of the day. Come in then if you must; perhaps I can find you a sandwich." She turned away to the kitchen with a smile. "Have a seat there at the table," she waved to the dining room.

He followed her to the kitchen door and watched her bustle about, slicing bread and ham.

"Must you stand there and watch me?"

"It's why I came." She reddened a bit at the back of her neck. He smiled.

"I thought it was for lunch."

"It was. Lunch with you."

"There you go, running off at that glib tongue of yours. Should anyone hear you, Lord knows what they might think."

"Do you care?"

She slathered butter on bread as if annoyed. Sunlight spilled through the kitchen window, firing her hair and bathing house dress, apron, and kerchief all in a golden glow.

"It's the principle of the thing. Room comes with board. Board is two meals a day, breakfast and supper. Lunch isn't on the bill of fare."

"It's always a principle of one sort or another with you."

"I have my rules."

"Like no fraternizing with guests."

"A good rule that was, too." She poured two glasses of tea and handed both to him. "Be of some use while you're here. Take these to the dining room." She gathered the plates of ham sandwiches, each with a scoop of potato salad.

He did as he was told, trailing over his shoulder, "You've allowed me to take you to supper a time or two. Has all that wretched fraternization violated you somehow?"

Behind him, green eyes glittered. She suppressed a smile.

"Tiz only I'm uncomfortable with it."

"Comfort, yes; I believe we've discussed that." He held a chair for her.

"Sit there now and eat your lunch before you while away the whole of my afternoon."

He sat and caught her eye. "There-in lies the problem."

"What problem?"

"Comfort. I am, and you're not."

"So you say, along with every other lass in a petticoat. Now eat your lunch."

Boots sounded on the steps, followed by a knock at the door.

"Now who could that be?"

Longstreet watched her go. Muffled voices sounded from the foyer. Maddie reappeared, followed by Cane.

"Look what the cat dragged in," she teased.

"Sorry to interrupt, Beau."

"Nothing to interrupt," she said.

"The Colonel got a job for us?" Beau said.

"He does. We're on our way to San Francisco. I'll fill you in while you pack."

"The comings and goings of your kind." She shook her head. "Have you had lunch, Mr. Cane?"

He shook his head.

"Can't travel on an empty stomach. Sit there. I haven't touched it."

"Much obliged, Mrs. O'Rourke. Kind of you to feed a stray cat."

She laughed. "Now there's a properly appreciative gentleman. You could take a lesson there, Mr. Longstreet."

She favored him with an exasperated glare.

He smiled and winked. "Miss me while I'm gone."

She rolled her eyes and stomped off to the kitchen. *I have my rules. I do.*

Denver

Pinkerton Office

Managing Director Reginald Kingsley stirred milk into a steaming cup of tea and placed the china saucer beside the morning folder on his impeccably neat desk. He took his seat, blew softly across the surface of his cup, and took a sip.

Little about him spoke of a Pinkerton operative, much less master detective. He had the pinched appearance of a librarian or college professor, with alert blue eyes, aquiline features, and a full moustache tinged with the barest hint of gray. He favored wool jackets of herringbone and tweed in subdued hues. When called for, he topped himself off in a stylish bowler, properly square to his head, now hung on a coat tree along with an umbrella at the corner of his spacious office. A silver-tipped cane leaned against the corner below. He carried the cane when called for. He might wield it as a baton or break it into a rapier-like blade. In the field, he armed himself with a short barreled .44 Colt pocket pistol cradled in a shoulder holster. He could disappear in a crowd, or turn himself out in a chameleon of disguise to suit his purpose. He dripped comfortable British charm, easily insinuating himself into the trust of the unsuspecting criminal or soon-to-be informant.

This morning, as was his custom, he opened the single folder on his desk to review his overnight correspondence. He flipped through several pages of routine head office memoranda before coming to rest on a somewhat more interesting item. Sixty thousand dollars in diamonds and assorted precious stones had a way of catching an investigator's attention. He finished the case report, eased himself out of his desk chair, and stuck his head out the office door to an outer office arrayed in rows of desks and filing cabinets, all bathed gray in winter morning light.

"I say, Trevor? A moment if you please."

An alert young man looked up from his desk. He followed Kingsley's summons up the aisle between desks. Tall and lean, he moved with the fluid grace of an athlete. Dark, wavy hair, deep-brown eyes, and crisply hewn features gave Trevor Trevane a rakishly handsome appearance. He possessed a keen mind, naturally suited to investigative work, with a ruthless streak that tended to violence when called for.

"Sir?"

"Have a seat." Kingsley fingered the dossier. "It seems we have a new client."

"Who would that be?"

"The Jeweler's Protective Union has engaged the agency."

"Jeweler's Protective Union? Never heard of it."

"Yes. It says here they represent member jewelers across the country to prevent, pursue, prosecute, and punish those who prey on their members." He slid the report across the desk.

Trevane scanned it with a soft whistle. "Sixty thousand dollars?"

"Quite an extraordinary haul and not easily disposed of I should think."

"San Francisco. The culprit could have hopped a ship and be well on his way to anywhere in the world by now."

"Certainly a possibility; but I rather think not."

"Why so?"

The corners of Kingsley's evenly trimmed moustache lifted ever so slightly to crinkle the corners of his eyes. "Call it a hunch."

"What do you propose we do?"

"Put the word out for starters. Let our usual network of informants know of our interest. It should be well worth the while of anyone who may be able to help us."

"I'll get on it straight away."

"I thought so."

CHAPTER FOUR

San Francisco

Cane and Longstreet stepped down from the hansom cab to the cobbled street. Cane paid the driver, who clucked to his horse and clattered away. Little commerce disturbed this quiet, shabby section of Montgomery Street a short distance from the bustling warrens of Chinatown. The dingy storefront where the cabby deposited them featured nothing more remarkable than a tarnished sign proclaiming International Imports.

"Sixty thousand in jewels . . . who would have guessed to look for a sum like that here?" Longstreet said.

"Somebody thought to. Somebody who likely knew where to look." Cane led the way inside.

Yellow morning light seeped through grime-streaked windows to a worn wooden counter separating visitors from a sparsely furnished office space. A slight, older man with a riot of disheveled white hair and a jeweler's loupe on his forehead sat at a desk with a crisply tailored visitor. The visitor rose.

"Mr. Cane, Mr. Longstreet? Montegue Malthus, Claims Special Agent, Comprehensive Insurance Company." He extended his hand and showed them through the counter gate. "This is Charles Furgeson, our client."

By the time Longstreet finished introduction amenities, Cane's attention was already drawn to the remains of a Chubb Lilly safe with hinges lacking a door. A newer model stood next to it. Malthus took note.

"I persuaded Charles not to remove it until you had a chance to examine it."

Cane nodded, crossed the office, and knelt beside the damaged safe. He rubbed his fingers along the door chase above the hinges and sniffed the result.

"Soup."

"Soup?" Malthus said.

"Nitroglycerin. Professional box man did this job."

"Box man?" Furgeson said.

"Professional safe cracker." Cane nodded at the new safe. "Hoping to have better results with this one?"

The jeweler nodded.

"Good luck. My advice? Smaller inventory."

"If he blew the safe, didn't someone hear it?" Longstreet said.

Malthus knit his brows. "Most certainly."

"Didn't anyone call the police?"

"There were quite a lot of explosions that night. The Chinese are quite fond of fireworks when it comes to celebrating their new year."

"And our box man knew his business," Cane said. "Ever been robbed before, Mr. Furgeson?"

"No, sir, I'm pleased to say."

"Were the contents of your safe typical of your inventory?"

"What do you mean by typical?"

"Sixty thousand dollars in gems seems rather a lot."

"I suppose it would be on the larger side of what we do; but we are a wholesale importer. Our inventory levels fluctuate."

"Unfortunate timing then," Longstreet said.

"Yes, I suppose you could say that."

"Is there anyone besides yourself, Mr. Furgeson, who knew you had so large an inventory in stock?" Cane said.

Furgeson pursed his lips in thought, then shook his head. "I can't think of anyone."

"A supplier perhaps?" Longstreet said.

"I buy from several sources, usually in much smaller quantities than this."

"What about a customer. Did anyone place an unusually large order recently?"

"I've enjoyed longstanding relationships with my customers. Their orders are quite steady. I can't say anything of late is out of the ordinary."

"So, it looks like our professional box man hit it big," Cane said.

"Have you any further questions, gentlemen?" Malthus said.

"Not at present," Cane said. "We'll be in touch as soon as we have anything."

Longstreet and Cane left the shop. Malthus followed them out to the street.

"I believe I can assist you with your line of inquiry."

"Oh?" Cane said.

"Insurance fraud was my first suspicion. I've conducted that enquiry. I don't believe Mr. Furgeson had anything to do with his loss."

"Had to ask," Cane said.

"Of course," Malthus said.

Longstreet eyed his partner. "So where does that leave us?"

"Loot like that needs to be fenced," Cane said.

"Know any fences in the neighborhood?"

"Not just any fence, either. Loot like that needs a fence who can handle the heat."

"Which fence might that be?"

"I don't know. But I know somebody who probably does."

"Who?"

"They call him the Cutter."

"Where do we find this Cutter?"

Cane smiled. "San Quentin."

Denver

The shabby coat, battered hat, stained britches, and dirty boots suited the rough and tumble clientele in the backstreet saloon. Trevane couldn't disguise his height, but he did his best to blend into the scene and deflect attention away from himself with a slouched posture and a shuffling gait. He took in the scene from the batwings.

Tobacco smoke hung in a yellow haze, flavored in stale beer and unwashed humanity. His gaze penetrated the gloom to a back-corner table where a solitary figure nursed a near-empty bottle alone. Trevane shuffled to the bar. He signaled the bartender with an ugly scar for a bottle and glass. He tossed an eagle to the man, who doubled as bouncer, took the bottle, and sidled off to the corner table.

The man took in the bottle, showed brown-stained yellow teeth, and nodded to a chair at the table.

"Slumming?"

Trevane filled the man's glass and poured one for himself. "Looking for information."

"Always. What can the Weasel do for you?"

"I'm looking for someone who's selling."

"Everybody sells something."

Trevane glanced around and lowered his voice. "Diamonds."

The man lifted a bushy brow and scratched a scruffy beard with dirty, cracked nails. "How many?"

"A lot of them."

"What's it worth?"

"Usual viper spiff. Fifty for a finger."

"You must want this seller bad."

Trevane slid a five-dollar gold piece across the table. "I'll throw in the bottle."

The Weasel scooped up the coin.

"You know where to find me."

He nodded, held up his glass, and tossed off his drink.

CHAPTER FIVE

San Quentin

They called it The Rock for a reason: a massive, three-story, stone-block structure barred in iron and surrounded on three sides by the waters of San Francisco Bay. Fog rolled across steel-gray waves, adding ominous foreboding to an austere edifice. Cane and Longstreet stepped down from their hired carriage to the cobbled, circular entry drive. Longstreet's gaze traveled up the façade to a rolling bank of leaden-gray cloud.

"Get locked up in there, you stay locked up," Longstreet said.

"So they say."

Cane led the way up the steps to the guarded front gate.

"Briscoe Cane and Beau Longstreet to see Warden Johnson."

The blue uniformed guard checked his appointment list. He removed a heavy ring of keys from his belt and opened the barred gate. A second guard appeared from a small guardhouse office beside the gate.

"Are you gentlemen armed?"

Longstreet opened his coat and handed his pistol to the gatekeeper. Cane handed over his back-up Forehand & Wadsworth before unbuckling his Colt rig with its sheathed blade. He handed the rig over along with the second blade taken from his left boot. The guard gathered the weapons and treated Cane to a scowl.

"This one's a damned arsenal."

"Follow me please, gentlemen." The second guard led them across an inner courtyard to a stairway leading to the entrance of an administrative building. A third guard unlocked a barred door at the top of the stairs to admit them. The steel door clanged closed behind them, the sound followed by a noticeable chill. The guard led them down a long, cold, stone corridor to a spacious office staffed by another uniformed officer.

"The warden will be with you in a few minutes."

"Home sweet home," Longstreet said.

"I'll take the Silver Slipper." Cane conjured up the picture of his third-rate saloon haunt back in Denver.

"For once, I agree with you."

A distinguished gentleman wearing a dark suit appeared in the office door.

"Gentlemen, James Johnson. How may I be of service?"

"Governor, Briscoe Cane. My partner here is Beau Long-street."

"Actually, it's Lieutenant Governor, but thank you for notic-ing. Most people don't. Lieutenant governors don't have much to do when the governor is in good health. In California they send us off to warden San Quentin. Now what can I do for you?"

"We represent the Great Western Detective League."

"Ah, yes; I believe we have one or two of yours in custody here."

"We'd like to interview one of them in connection with a case we are investigating."

"And that would be?"

"Jubal Craven."

"The Cutter. Are you working on the International Imports case?"

"As a matter of fact we are. How did you know?"

"Sixty thousand dollars in diamonds gets people's attention

in a little town like San Francisco. What makes you think Craven can help? We've kept pretty close tabs on his whereabouts."

Longstreet chuckled. "It would appear so."

"Jailhouse humor. I am curious, though."

"We're interested in some of his former associates," Cane said.

"Makes sense. Simpson, show these men to the interrogation cell, and see that Craven is brought to them. Is there anything else you might require?"

"No, sir."

"Pleasure meeting you both. Good luck. We've got room for the perpetrator if you catch him."

The interrogation cell suited the purpose. It was two cells really. The interrogators were locked in a room with a small holding cell on one wall with a door leading to a passageway somehow connected to the cell blocks. The cell contained a single wooden chair bolted to the floor. The interrogation room offered the comforts of two wooden chairs and a table, not bolted to the floor. Presently a guard admitted Jubal Craven, clad in striped pajamas, into the holding cell.

"Wave when you're finished. I'll be watching." The guard closed the door.

"Cane, what brings you to these luxurious accommodations?" The Cutter said as he took his seat.

"A case I thought you might be able to help with."

"Out of the goodness of my heart."

"How about a kind word to the warden."

"You can do better than that."

"Let's see if you can help first."

"You're interested in the International Imports heist."

"Word travels fast."

"Small prison."

"The box man used soup."

"I'm impressed. Not many do."

"Any idea who might be in the area?"

"Hard to say. I've kind of lost touch with my contacts, so to speak."

"Small prison," Longstreet said.

"Smart ass."

"We try."

"Let's try a different approach," Cane said. "Diamonds and precious stones need to be fenced. Let's say one of your former customers had come into such a windfall; where would he go to unload the merchandise?"

"None of the usual suspects handles that kind of merchandise."

"I didn't think so. So where would your former customer go?"

Craven shifted in his chair, glancing left and right. "Sometimes these walls have ears. What's it worth to you?"

"A hundred would keep you in the makin's for a spell."

"A hundred fifty."

"If the information is good."

"The Don."

"The Don. Who is this Don?" Longstreet said.

"No one knows. All I know is he runs an organization that can handle that kind of merchandise."

"How do you find this Don?"

"You don't. His people find you."

"Where do his people find you?" Cane asked.

"Cheyenne, Santa Fe, sometimes Denver."

"And they just drop in on the unsuspecting jewel thief."

He shook his head. "You got to let them know you're selling. You put the word out."

"The word, like 'I have a fortune in hot stones'?"

"No." He lowered his voice. "The word you're looking for *El Anillo.*"

Longstreet cut his eyes to Cane. Cane nodded.

"A hundred fifty, Cutter."

Craven smiled. "Pleasure doing business with you."

CHAPTER SIX

Shady Grove

I paused, pencil over pad. "*El Anillo*—weren't they implicated in the case of those bogus bonds?"

"They were. If you recall, the big fish got away. We didn't know him for this mysterious Don at the time, but the Cutter's information proved both accurate and valuable."

"Time for lunch, Colonel."

My Penny. Sometimes it still surprised me I thought of her so. It spoke much of how far we'd come in the span of two short years. She still took my breath away even in her pale-blue uniform dress with the little white apron. The soft form of a woman's figure could not be denied by the severity of her dress. She composed her pretty lips in the hint of a smile reminiscent of the famous Mona Lisa painting. She wore her dark hair curled short beneath the crown of a nurse's cap. Her eyes were as soft as melted chocolates filled with caramel. She had a velvety voice with the hint of an Irish brogue dipped in butterscotch. A throaty laugh crinkled the sprinkle of freckles on the bridge of a turned-up nose. A light scent of vanilla ice cream flavored her presence.

"Lunch?"

The Colonel lurched me back to the present.

"Please . . . the remains of yesterday evening's burnt offering more like it. You couldn't put it to taste at the first feeding, never mind a warmed-over second attempt."

"Oh, come now, Colonel, you haven't wasted away yet."

"Not from the lack of proper nourishment. I feel I must be waning."

"You can't go off and wane on me," I protested. "We have a new case to solve."

"Then intercede in my feeding. You do have some influence with this girl and me to thank for it. See if you can't persuade her to permit us some other accommodation."

It was true. The old scoundrel summoned up my courage for me in introducing me to my girl whilst I was too tongue-tied to speak on my own behalf.

"And, further, I presume you have far more interesting plans for the rest of this Saturday than my best hope for a nap."

"A motion picture show and a stroll home after a sundae."

"I knew it. I'm left to gruel and a nap preceding yet another helping of gruel, whilst you two enjoy the rest of the day. Can you not at least spare me one portion of inferior cuisine?"

"Colonel, you know your nutrition is carefully monitored for your own good."

"Nutrition she calls it. Nutrition, can you believe it?"

I shrugged.

Penny rolled her eyes. "Come along now, Colonel. We shan't be late for lunch."

She wheeled him away grumbling to himself. I watched. *A ring with a stone? A ring without a stone?*

Denver

He'd put out the word as his informant suggested. The saloon was a back-street dump. The bartender, a grizzled brute in need of a bath, nodded and gave him a bottle and glass. He'd come back each night for the last three to wait. He looked and felt out of place. Broad shouldered with a barrel chest and narrow waist, Duval looked as though he'd been hewn out of a large block of black granite. He had fine features composed of a stoic expression accented by a well-formed skull devoid of hair. He had luminous dark eyes and even, white teeth. He spoke in a deep, resonant tone flavored with a Cajun French accent. He wore a black suit with fine white linen and matching ribbon tie. A derby bowler perched at a jaunty angle. Finely forged chain fastened a silver pocket watch to his belt. He wore a brace of ivory handled, short barreled Colts in a shoulder rig. He also favored a sawed-off double barrel 10-gauge shotgun, yet his weapons of choice most often formed in the fists of massive black hands. Those hands could wield a lock pick with the skill of a surgeon or deftly manage a vial of nitroglycerin. The sordid refuse that made up the saloon's clientele left him alone. Any man fool enough to come into a place like this turned out like that had to be lethal. The 10-gauge lying on the table beside his bottle spoke all the warning required.

He'd finished his second drink when the skinny, pockmarked Mexican approached his table.

"I understand you seek us."

"El Anillo?"

"Sí."

"Have a seat." He turned to signal the bartender only to find the man at his elbow with a bottle of tequila and a glass.

"Gracias." He poured for the bartender to depart. "How may we be of service, *señor* . . . ?"

"Duval. And you are?"

"Escobar."

"How do I know you are who you say you are?"

"I got your message. I work for the Don."

"That's it?"

"Take it or no."

"I have merchandise."

"What sort of merchandise?"

"Diamonds and precious stones."

Ferret face lifted a brow. "How much?"

"Sixty thousand."

"From San Francisco."

Duval nodded. "Can your Don move it?"

The man laughed and tossed off his drink.

"I will speak with the Don. You will hear from us within the week."

Bright eyes in a dark corner followed the Mexican out the door.

Denver Cemetery
Midnight
Trevane crunched up a stone path to the wrought-iron gate. The gate opened with a shriek in the stillness fit for a wail from the crypt. A stone path wound its way among the tombstones by the light of a fingernail moon and a blanket of stars. *Hell of a place for a meeting. Why?*

The informant waited nervously by a freshly dug grave.

"Is this really necessary?" Trevane said by way of greeting.

"It is."

"Why?"

"*El Anillo* has eyes and ears everywhere."

"*El Anillo* . . . what the hell is that?"

"The ring of the Don."

"What Don?"

"No one knows."

"You're talking in riddles, Weasel. What have you got?"

"Your diamond seller, I think."

"What makes you think so?"

"He met with one of the Don's men."

"So?"

"So, if a man had the sort of merchandise you describe, *El*

Anillo is one of the few that might move it."

"I see. Who is this man?"

"Big black hombre. Sounds foreign."

"Does he have a name?"

"I followed him to the Palace Hotel. They called him Mr. Duval."

Trevane smiled.

"Do you have it?" The Weasel held out his hand.

Five double eagles clattered into his hand, glinting in low light.

CHAPTER SEVEN

Shady Grove
Saturday
I preceded the Colonel to the veranda the following week. A sullen bank of gray cloud rolled over the front-range peaks, threatening a storm. I wondered at the wisdom of moving inside to the solarium as Penny wheeled the Colonel out to join me. We exchanged smiles.

"There you two go again running away with your romance as though I serve no more useful purpose than giving you leave to see one another during working hours."

"And good day to you too, Colonel," I said. "Speaking of good day, perhaps we should move into the solarium."

"Why ever for?"

I looked to the sky by way of reply. He followed my glance.

"For a few clouds?"

"For a storm."

"Rubbish. What storm? Moisten your pencil; we've a story to tell."

I shrugged.

Penny rolled her eyes. "I shall be back if it rains."

With that she was off.

"Now, where were we?"

"The Cutter . . ."

"Ah, yes, Jubal Craven. Cane and Longstreet returned from San Francisco convinced the stolen diamonds would lead us to

41

the criminal ring that managed to elude us in the bond forgery case. I alerted league members in Cheyenne and Santa Fe along with our own local law enforcement members to be on the lookout for anyone attempting to sell precious stones and the ferret-faced operative who was our only known connection to the mysterious crime syndicate. As is often the case with investigations such as these, we were then left to await further developments."

Denver

She'd come to recognize his foot fall on the porch step. She shook her head in exasperation at a small involuntary flutter of excitement. *Foolish girl!* She primped an errant strand of hair in her reflection at the kitchen window. The front door opened.

"It's only the wayward traveler," Longstreet called.

She poked her head out of the kitchen. "Wayward, now there's a truer word ever spoken."

"You did miss me."

"Don't be too sure."

"Wouldn't dream of it."

"And I suppose you've missed your supper as well," she said, glancing at the clock.

Beau raised his hands in mock surrender. "I know, I know. I've missed the appointed hour."

"Can't have a resident fainting from hunger. T' would be unseemly. We've a pot roast. I can fix you a cold sandwich slice."

"Ah, Maddie dear, you're an angel of mercy."

"Don't interpret my kindness for endearment."

"Heaven forfend."

"Have a seat. I'll only be a minute."

He pulled out his usual chair next to hers at the head of the table. By the time she came from the kitchen carrying his plate he was seated with a bottle of sherry on the table.

"What's that?"

"Sherry. I brought it to celebrate my return home. I know your policy as regards strong spirits, but I thought you might make a small exception for so cultured a libation on so special an occasion."

"Special are we?"

"If you say so."

She feigned a frown. Opened a cupboard at the sideboard and produced two crystal glasses. Beau poured. He lifted his glass.

"To small exceptions."

"You are that."

He touched her glass. She took a sip and smiled in spite of herself.

"So, did you find your diamonds in San Francisco?"

He shook his head around a mouthful of roast beef. "No; but we think we may have a connection to the gang that was behind that bond forgery case last year."

"Really? They must be quite industrious."

"Quite. Any news about here?"

"The usual."

"Good. Then no erstwhile suitors have come along in my absence."

Piqued. "What earthly business would such a thing be of yours?"

"Just looking after my interests. Here . . . let me top that up for you." He poured. He noticed she let him.

"Your interests, is it. Your interests run to skirts. I suspect you had a woman waiting in every depot stop betwixt Cheyenne and San Francisco."

"You wound me. Though I do enjoy the wee hint of jealousy. A little green goes nicely with your eyes."

"You are impossible, Beau Longstreet."

He wiped a last bit of gravy from his lips on his napkin. "I assure you, I am eminently possible."

She gathered his plate.

"Shall we take our sherry to the parlor?"

She paused at the kitchen door. "I don't know that I'm comfortable with that."

"I am." He picked up the bottle and their glasses on the way to the parlor settee.

She appeared in the parlor entry. "You know this sort of familiarity is against my better judgement."

"I assure you, I'm a far better judge when it comes to familiarity."

"I was afraid of that." She took a seat beside him, a discreet distance away.

He handed her a freshly filled glass. "How much longer must we maintain this little charade?"

"What charade?"

"The charade that pretends you feel nothing between us."

"I don't know what you're talking about."

"Oh, but you do. The pink in your cheeks and that little pulse in your neck tell no lie."

She put her hands to her cheeks. "It's only the sherry."

"Is it?" Slowly he leaned across the great divide separating them. Her eyes, liquid green, drifted behind lazy lids. He caught her lips in his, ever so lightly. He felt her yield ever so slightly.

"See, I told you it was a charade."

"I'm comfortable with that. I'm not comfortable with . . . this." Another kiss, more fulsome this time. She pulled back.

"It's time for me to go to my room before . . ."

"Before what?"

"Before it gets any . . . later."

She was gone. Longstreet smiled after her.

Pinkerton Office

"Looks like we have something." Trevane stood in the office

door, silhouetted in morning sun.

"What's that?" Kingsley gestured to a side chair.

"One of our vipers spotted a known fence talking business."

"Fences do business every day."

"Not this one, according to our source. It's some sort of syndicate. Calls itself *El Anillo.*"

"The Ring."

"Our boy is scared to death of them. He insisted we meet in the cemetery at midnight."

"Seriously? Why ever for?"

"The very walls he says have eyes and ears when it comes to that syndicate."

"*El Anillo* has a familiar ring to it." He curled the tip of his moustache in thought. "Cane took down a suspect in the bond caper. The charges as I recall mentioned something about a crime syndicate by that name. Didn't hold him long. Jumped bail before he ever went to trial. So, our viper thinks they're involved in the diamond heist."

"Sure enough to do his informing in a cemetery at midnight."

"Who's the seller?"

"Black man. Name's Duval. He's staying at the Palace."

"High rent."

"Judging by his style, he can afford it."

"You have him under surveillance?"

He nodded.

"When do we move in?"

"When he delivers."

"Very good, Trevor. Keep me informed."

CHAPTER EIGHT

Santa Fe

El Patrón, Don Victor Carnicero, stood on a tiled patio beyond double doors to his library. The late rays of sun fired mountain tops orange in the west. He fingered his neatly trimmed white goatee, contemplating the coded telegram from Escobar. Sixty thousand dollars in untraceable diamonds and precious stones made a tempting prize. What to do with it? Across the large formal library warmed in candle glow behind him, a muscular mountain of a bodyguard with an ugly scar awaited his reply. The literary collection suited Carnicero's pretense of legitimacy. The Don carried himself with patrician bearing and an aura of power that suggested a larger stature than his average height. Handsome still in the echo of youthful vigor, waves of white hair set off a swarthy complexion with the patina of polished leather. He filled a room with the presence of a benevolent grandfather were it not for his eyes. Deep set and black, they glittered with an inner fire that smoldered in equanimity or enflamed in rage. Little ruffled his outward demeanor. Only his eyes gave light to a ruthless hard edge.

He presided over a shadowy network known to the very few as *El Anillo.* His organization discreetly served the indelicate needs of the rich and powerful. His clients included crooked politicians, organized labor, robber baron industrialists, affluent anarchists, and high-stakes criminals. His specialties included murder for hire, protection, and liquidation of illegal merchandise, all performed in a manner designed to strictly assure his clients' anonymity as well as his own. All his services came at exorbitant fees as befitted the risks he took and his clients' means of payment.

The question at hand of course: what to do with a fortune in stolen jewels? He smiled to himself. The question didn't matter. A suitable opportunity would present itself. He sat at his desk and scratched out coded instructions to Escobar.

Palace Hotel

Denver

They sat at a quiet corner table in the hotel salon, the waiter compensated to see to it they were not disturbed. Polished dark wood and candlelit, leather-covered furnishings gave an aura of elegance and legitimacy to the matter at hand.

"Twenty thousand." Escobar drew on a thin black cheroot and expelled a cloud of blue smoke.

Duval bunched his brows, not quite believing what he'd just heard. "I thought you'd take all of it."

"*Sí*. All of it for twenty thousand."

"That's but a third of its worth. Forty thousand would be fair."

"Distribution is risky and expensive."

"So is cracking boxes. Let's split the difference—thirty thousand."

The ferret inspected the burning tip of his cigarillo. "Twenty-five. Take it or leave it."

"I'm being robbed."

"And your point?"

"When can you accept delivery?"

"Give me two days," the *El Anillo* man said.

"Very well."

Pinkerton Office

Late-afternoon sun turned the office golden. Trevane's shadow darkened Kingsley's door.

"It's time. They met again today."

"Did they make an exchange?"

"No. I suspect that is next. If we want a clean recovery of the jewels we need to make our pinch soon."

"Tonight then."

Palace Hotel

Duval stared into the darkened ceiling. The faint glow of street lamps seeped through lace curtains. Twenty-five thousand was a pittance. Scarcely worth the risk of handling enough juice to blow the box. What was to be done about it? Turn a larger profit? But how? The glimmer of an idea pricked at the back of his mind. Greed. That was it. Much could be done with greed. A soft "click" snapped him awake.

The door burst open. Lantern light shattered the darkness. Shadowed men with guns filled the room.

"Pinkerton! You're under arrest."

Someone swept his guns off the nightstand.

"On what charge?"

"Grand theft."

"Grand theft what?"

"Sixty thousand dollars in precious jewels taken from International Imports of San Francisco, to be precise. Now sit up. Hands in the air."

He did as he was told, his mind racing. "Pinkerton, you said. Who's in charge?"

"That would be me, Reginald Kingsley," a tweed-coated gentleman in a bowler said. "Now where are the stones?"

Someone lit the bedside lamp.

"That necessitates a conversation. As you might imagine, I

don't have them with me."

"All right then. Converse."

"In private."

"You forfeited your privacy privileges when you blew that box."

"Not if you want those jewels back."

Kingsley met his gaze. He had an idea where this was headed. "Trevane, stay with me and keep our friend here covered. The rest of you, wait in the hall." The room cleared. "That's as much privacy as you get. Now what's on your mind?"

"A deal."

"What sort of deal?"

"You recover half the stones, and I walk."

"Why would I entertain such a deal when I have you in custody?"

"Because the stones are worth more than I am, and, as of now, you have none of them."

"Perhaps not; but I believe with enough—shall we say, encouraging—interrogation, you'll happily lead us to them."

"Don't be too sure about that. There's a plantation overseer in Georgia who thought that. He ended up dead."

"You're in a poor position to threaten me; you just confessed to murder."

"He thought I was in a poor position, too. Now let's be practical. Thirty thousand is a princely recovery. Pinkerton is known among thieves to make such arrangements from time to time. It is how the firm gets some of its most valuable informants. You do know who my buyer is. Thirty thousand is a handsome reward for a prize such as that."

Silence spread like a pool across the floor between them.

Duval smiled to himself. *He had them.*

CHAPTER NINE

Velvet Ribbon
Denver

Duval found the stately Victorian on a secluded side street. A bow of lavender velvet ribbon tied about the whitewashed door post identified the house. He climbed the broad porch fronting the house to a massive center entrance. He tapped the shiny brass knocker. The door swung open to a polished wood foyer lit by a large cut-crystal chandelier. A stunningly attractive, dark-eyed woman dressed in a satin gown greeted him.

"Welcome to the Velvet Ribbon, Monsieur Duval." She closed the door behind him. "I am Marie Ambrochette, madam here," she said with a nod. "*Señor* Escobar has not come down yet. He asked that I make you comfortable in a private salon. This way, if you please."

She led the way past an elegantly furnished parlor rendered all the more beautiful by the exquisitely attractive women who greeted him with an appraising glance or a smile. A polished corridor passed rows of wood-paneled doors to the one she opened for him.

"Carmel will be in to take your refreshment order. I will inform *Señor* Escobar you have arrived."

The room was candlelit and furnished with a settee and wing chairs upholstered in matching dark green. They clustered around a low table festooned with a vase of fresh flowers beside a cheery fireplace. A lovely oriental rug brought the room together in tasteful earth tones. The door had no more than closed when a soft rap sounded.

"Come in."

The girl smiled. Dark hair, dark eyes, skin the color of creamed coffee, dressed in a tastefully provocative oriental gown.

"What would *monsieur* care for?"

Her voice barely rose above a whisper. Duval knew at once. Then again, he had business to discuss. "Perhaps a glass of sherry."

She favored him with a pretty pout and disappeared. She returned moments later with a silver tray containing a decanter of sherry, a bottle of tequila, and two glasses. She set it on the table.

"Should you require anything further . . ." Eyelids dipped. She lifted a delicate chin to a velvet cord hanging unobtrusively in a corner by the door. ". . . just ring." With that she was gone.

Just ring. Duval poured himself a glass of sherry, as Escobar barged into the room.

"I hope you have found everything to your satisfaction."

"Of course, but, then again, I've only just arrived."

Escobar poured tequila and took a seat. "You have the stones?"

Duval drew two leather sacks from his pockets and laid them on the table.

Escobar spilled some of the contents of one into the palm of his hand. Diamonds glittered in the soft lamp light picking up all the colors of the rainbow in their facets. He looked up expectantly.

"Where are the rest?"

"I encountered a small problem."

"What sort of problem?"

"A Pinkerton problem."

"Pinkerton?"

"They arrested me two nights ago."

"How is it that you escaped?"

"I didn't. I bought my way out."

"With half our jewels."

"Your jewels?"

"We had a deal. Sixty thousand in gems."

"Stolen for twenty-five thousand in cash, which I have yet to receive."

"You don't seriously expect us to pay you for merchandise you cannot deliver. That, I assure you, is the least of your worries."

"My worries. What do you mean?"

"The Don will not be pleased. You shall see; he does not suffer disappointment agreeably. I will do my best to see that these purchase his indulgence."

"What if I could show your Don how to turn these thirty thousand in stones into a true fortune?"

Escobar laughed. Tossed off his drink and poured another.

"I'm not joking."

"And how would my *Patrón* come by this fortune you promise?"

Duval held up the unopened sack. "By selling the mine these came from."

The ferret's gaze went cold. "You know how to do this?"

"*Oui.*"

"We?"

"*Sí.*"

The Mexican fingered his moustache, drew a cheroot from his coat pocket, and lit it with a candle. "This may beg my *Patrón*'s indulgence. I make no promises. I will take these stones and your boast to him. Meet me in Santa Fe in two weeks. Be there, or you sign your own death warrant."

"Where shall I meet you in Santa Fe?"

"We will find you. One more thing, *amigo*. If you are lying about this, I will personally terminate our arrangement. *Comprende?*"

San Francisco

It made for quite an entourage. Tobias Livingston, executive director of the Jeweler's Protective Union insisted on it. He personally led the delegation up a sun-washed Montgomery Street to International Imports. Kingsley followed, accompanied by two Pinkerton agents, providing security for the recovered jewels. Bright sunlight muted to a dirty glow inside the dingy office reception area. Livingston presented his credentials to Charles Furgeson, proprietor, and Montegue Malthus, claims special agent for Comprehensive Insurance Company.

"May I present Reginald Kingsley, managing director of the Pinkerton Agency's Denver office."

Kingsley exchanged handshakes with Furgeson and Malthus. Livingston beamed.

"As you know, Mr. Furgeson, the Jeweler's Protective Union was formed to protect the interests of our members' security. To that end we contracted with the Pinkerton Agency to prevent, pursue, prosecute, and punish those who prey on our members. Our program has resulted in a partial recovery of your recent loss. Mr. Kingsley, if you would, please do the honors."

Kingsley placed a leather sack on the counter. "We judge the recovery to be approximately half of your reported loss, subject to your verification, of course. We understand this does not complete the assignment. I can assure you that every resource of the Pinkerton Eye That Never Sleeps is dedicated to a complete recovery of your merchandise."

Furgeson emptied the contents of the bag onto a black velvet cloth, running an appraising eye over the glittering stones.

"We are grateful to you gentlemen for your efforts on our behalf. With Mr. Malthus's assistance, we shall begin our inventory forthwith to establish our recovery against the original loss."

"Mr. Kingsley, if I may?" Malthus said. "What can you tell me of the circumstances by which you recovered these stones, and, more particularly, what might have become of the perpetrator and the remainder of our loss?"

"We encountered the perpetrator in the act of soliciting a fence for stolen merchandise. The alleged fence was in fact a Pinkerton informant under surveillance in connection with another case. When our agents moved in, the man we believe to be your perpetrator escaped. These stones happened to be in the possession of our informant at the time."

"I see. It would appear we are the beneficiary of fortuitous circumstances," Malthus said.

"Fortuitous indeed." Kingsley smiled.

"Did the fugitive leave any trace that might give us hope for further recovery?"

"It was dark. Our men didn't get a good look at him, though our informant is cooperating with the investigating agents. He tells us the perpetrator is a black man, likely of Cajun descent. I assure you we will notify the Jeweler's Protective Union the moment we have further progress to report."

"Yes . . . well then, we've only to pin our hopes on that." Livingston beamed.

CHAPTER TEN

Shady Grove

Morning sun climbed to its pinnacle. The Colonel's narrative slowed as though he might be tiring. I sensed it time to wrap up this day's session.

"So, Pinkerton recovered half the loot and let the perpetrator go?"

"It certainly smelled that way and not just to me. Malthus had his own suspicions, or maybe it was just the fact his company was still out thirty thousand dollars in diamonds and gems. He said as much when he notified us the thief was a black Cajun."

"But wouldn't that be unethical on Kingsley's part?"

"One of the things that made Pinkerton so bloody effective in those days was their network of informants. They used them most efficiently just as we used our league members. One was always left to wonder how all those well-connected miscreants were recruited. I believe there was more to it than small spiffs . . ."

This last trailed off in a racking dry cough. I waited for the spasm to pass.

"May I get you some water?"

He shook his head. "Just the damn ague."

"Perhaps we should go inside. It is a bit chilly out here today."

"Nonsense! I'll not be treated like some hot-house orchid."

"Of that you shall never be accused."

He laughed and coughed.

My Penny came to fetch him for lunch. A note of concern in her eye as she saw the cough rack him. Our eyes met. The cough passed.

"Time for lunch, Colonel."

He scowled. "That won't be necessary, my dear. I've persuaded my good friend Robert here to take me out for lunch and a beer. You remember our Robert, don't you?"

She blushed. I liked it.

"As a matter of fact, there are two reasons Robert won't be taking you along on any such outing. First are the rules you very well know, and, second, we're off to a matinee and supper."

"Rules be damned. Take me along. I can nap in a motion picture show as easily as I can here in my cell. I suspect your supper will come with ice cream for dessert, which is a good deal more than anything I shall be treated to in the culinary ambiance of our refectory, as you call it. Re-factory seems more to the point."

"It tis'nt we wouldn't welcome your witty companionship, but rules are rules, and I have no authority to dispense with them."

"How about we make a break for it? It's done all the time in jails."

"Come now, Colonel. Shady Grove isn't as bad as jail."

"Says you. You see what I'm up against here, Robert?"

She wheeled him away.

"We'll discuss my escape next week."

Santa Fe

Santa Fe nestled in the foothills at the southern tip of the Sangre De Cristo Mountains on the banks of the Santa Fe River. Church spires and adobe architecture gleamed against faultless blue sky, proclaiming the city's rich Hispanic and religious traditions. The center of governments past and present occupied the dusty corners of Lincoln and Palace Avenues. The single-story adobe-and-tile Mexican Palace held the northwest corner beside the quadrangle known as the Government Corral to the west. The more recent two-story headquarters of the New Mexico territorial government stood on the opposite corner across Lincoln to the south.

Further to the north the stately, three-story Capitol Plaza Hotel dominated the middle of the block on the north side of Washington Street. Duval climbed the steps to a broad veranda fronting the hotel and stepped into the richly appointed candlelit lobby. The hotel dining room beyond the registration desk on the left had quieted after the busy dinner hour. A curved stairway ascended to the guest rooms past a dark-wood paneled salon. Settees and easy chairs upholstered in brocades of blue and green invited guests to the comforts of the salon for refreshments and quiet conversation. He crossed the lobby to the registration desk, boot heels clicking on the polished wooden floor.

"Good evening, sir. Welcome to the Capitol Plaza. How may we be of service?"

"A room."

The clerk opened the guest register. Duval signed *Horace Carousel*.

"Very good, Mr. . . . Carousel. And how long will you be staying with us?"

"Depends on my business. Let's say three nights for now."

"Very well. That will be three dollars." He passed a key across the counter. "Room two ten, top of the stairs. Enjoy your stay."

Duval deposited his traveling bag in a tastefully appointed room. He went down to the salon for a drink. By the time he returned to his room, he had a note under his door.

A carriage will pick you up tomorrow evening at six o'clock.

The sun drifted toward its setting on western peaks. Blue shadow lengthened along the tree lined avenue past the hotel's stately entrance. The carriage arrived promptly at six. The driver opened the door for Duval. Inside a brute of a man greeted him. The man filled half the carriage, physically intimidating even to a man of Duval's stature. He held out a black hood.

"Put it on."

"Why?"

"*Patrón* insists."

The carriage and its ugly brute disappeared inside the hood. The team lurched into motion, rocking and rolling into the night. Duval lost all sense of distance and direction inside the stifling hood. After more than an hour the carriage slowed to a stop. He could hear a muffled exchange of some sort followed by the creak of what he guessed to be some heavy gate. The carriage clattered over a cobblestone drive and drew to a halt.

"You may remove the hood."

Duval welcomed a lungful of fresh air. The brute climbed out of the carriage and stood beside the door. Duval stepped down to a spacious plaza at the entrance to a rambling adobe hacienda. Ornately carved double doors opened to another, somewhat less imposing, brute.

"This way."

Duval followed the man from a tiled foyer down a long hall softly lit by wall sconces. He was shown into a spacious library with a massive fireplace, lavishly furnished along with a massive desk hewn in Victorian counterpoint to the otherwise Hispanic influence surrounding it. The ferret Escobar rose from a chair.

"Have a seat. The Don will be with us momentarily."

"Nice place you've got here, wherever we are."

"Should we have a successful meeting, perhaps you will enjoy your stay enough to leave."

Another threat. Duval set aside his irritation with a strong sense these people were capable of backing them up. He thought the plan he prepared to propose to be sound. A hint of doubt nagged at him. *It better be.*

Boot heels tattooed the tile hall. The patrician known as *Patrón* swept into the room. Both men rose instinctively.

"So, this is the man who lost half of my precious stones. *Señor* Duval, I believe it is."

"My pleasure, Don Victor."

"We shall see about your pleasure." The Don took a wing chair beside the fireplace. "Have a seat. Now tell me about your plan to make me forget my losses for the gains we shall make on the remains."

Duval forced a smile as though he had not a care in the world. He spread his hands in a gesture of giving. "Quite simple really: we sell the mine from which these stones came."

"You are in possession of this mine?"

"Not yet."

"Where is this mine?"

"Wherever we put it."

"Don't talk in riddles. It annoys me."

"We use the stones we have to create the illusion of a rich mining claim. We syndicate the claim, selling shares to wealthy investors."

A dark light flickered recognition in Carnicero's eye. A slow smile lifted the corners of his moustache. He nodded. *"Bueno."* He clapped his hands. "Rodolfo! Tequila!"

One of the brutes appeared carrying a silver tray with a crystal decanter and glasses. Duval relaxed. He expected to leave. The Don passed glasses around.

"Salut." They tossed off the fiery liquor and refilled their glasses.

"Now, tell me more of this plan."

"We use some of the stones to attract investors. They will want to verify the find. We salt our claim with stones they can easily find to confirm our discovery. We sell them shares to raise the funds needed to develop the mine."

"And these monies far exceed my losses."

"Exactly."

"Who are these investors?"

"I don't know yet."

"No matter. I know an *hombre* who does. I think, too, we shall need more stones than we have. Escobar, put out the word to some of our friends: the Don is buying diamonds and jewels. A few humble robberies should provide more than enough. While you are at it, the informant who tipped Pinkerton off to my losses."

"The one known as the Weasel?"

"*Sí.* See that he is paid for his crime. Are you a mine expert, *Señor* Duval?"

He shrugged. "I crack safes."

"You shall need a partner who is. I have just the man in mind. Tonight, we return you to the hotel. Stay there. It will take a few days to make the necessary arrangements."

"As you wish, Don Victor."

CHAPTER ELEVEN

Denver

Midnight. The Weasel crunched up the cemetery path patched white in moonlight and scudding dark clouds. He shook his head. He supposed he had only himself to blame for the inconvenience. He'd asked the Pinkerton man to meet him here. It shouldn't come as a surprise the Pinkerton picked a return to this meeting place for whatever he had on his mind. The note came with a ten-dollar gold piece. Whatever he had on his mind it must be important. The crypt described in the note stood at the top of a small rise. Little description was needed for the largest memorial in the cemetery. No sign of the Pinkerton man. He settled into the shadows to wait.

Caught from behind in a vise like grip, a lightning like flash in the moonlight sliced across his throat. His scream cut short in a rush of hot air, gone dark in warm gush.

Pinkerton Office

Trevane stood at the office door framed in mid-morning light. Kingsley looked up from his second cup of tea.

"Have we a development?"

"You could say that. They found the Weasel this morning."

"The Weasel?"

"Our informant. Dead. Killed in a curious way."

"How so?"

"Throat cut, but here's the curious part. The killer took time to carve a word in his chest: *'silencio.'* "

"Silence. Sounds like the killer intended to send a message."

"There's more. The third finger of his left hand was cut off."

"The ring finger. *El Anillo.* Who do you suppose the message is for?"

"For us."

"Hmm." Kingsley stroked his chin. "I suppose it is."

Chicago

The dark-eyed gentleman known only as the Counselor unlocked the door to his room. He stepped inside and spotted the small, yellow envelope lying on the threadbare carpet. He tore the telegram open.

Service required in Cheyenne.

A telegram. The matter must be urgent. There could only be one sender of such a cryptic message. A disbarred lawyer, Counselor, as his employers knew him, understood the role he played representing his clients. He was an anonymous agent, a well-paid break in any chain of evidence that might link his clients to the crimes or less than ethical dealings he was paid to facilitate. Given his experience in such matters, he had proven himself able to evade detection, thereby providing his client and himself a further layer of protection.

He packed lightly for the morning train.

Capitol Plaza Hotel
Santa Fe

Duval sat alone at a quiet corner table in the salon. He savored the bouquet of a passable brandy, wondering when next the Don might move their project forward. A handsome young man turned out in an elegant gray suit approached his table.

"Monsieur Duval?"

He nodded.

"Jeremiah Endicott at your service." He extended a hand.

Duval returned the greeting with suspicion. "And what service is it you expect I might require?"

Endicott glanced about. "Mining experience. Our colleague sent me."

Duval took his hand. "Have a seat."

"How's the brandy?"

"Passable."

"I'll risk it." He signaled the waiter.

"Exactly what mining experience are we talking about?"

"I've a degree in geology. Spent a couple of years working for Comstock. Enough to learn the lingo and figure out you can't make any real money unless you own the mine. Our colleague thought my credentials ideally suited to the enterprise you propose."

"It would seem so. How are we to proceed?"

The waiter arrived with a brandy.

"I understand you have the initial stake."

Duval nodded.

"Our colleague is taking steps to identify prospective investors. We'll use your poke to entice them. In the meantime, we must stake out a claim for the mine. We need more findings for our investors to confirm. Our colleague is seeing to that procurement. It will be up to us to prepare the field and guide our investors to confirmation. Once the syndicate is closed, it will be up to the investors to develop it."

"Very smooth."

"The brandy?"

Duval scowled.

"Now about our working relationship," Endicott said. "I wasn't sure how to play this until I had the opportunity to meet you. I can see you are a refined gentleman. A cut above the usual actor in such a drama. I think your part might best be played as that of a gentleman's gentleman."

"I'm to be your valet?"

"Don't you see?"

"I see that I hatched this enterprise as you call it. Now I'm to play the part of your servant."

"No one will question it. Any other arrangement would require explanation. In this sort of deception, the less said the better. Let our investors' expectations speak for themselves. It may seem a trifle demeaning, but then again there's a bloody fortune to be paid for the part."

Duval glared. *Bloody fortune.*

"Your tie is crooked," Duval said.

"There's a good fellow." Endicott lifted his glass.

CHAPTER TWELVE

Cheyenne

Counselor took a room at the Union Pacific Hotel. The depot and adjacent red-light district could be noisy, but he didn't expect to be here long. Just long enough for the Don—or more likely the Don's representative—to contact him. The knock at his door came just after lunch on the day following his arrival. His caller, the beady-eyed killer, Escobar, and one of his evil smelling cheroots. He admitted his caller along with his foul-smelling habit to the confines of his small room.

"How may I be of service to your superior this time?"

"We seek investors to syndicate development of a mine."

"What sort of mine?"

"Diamonds and other precious stones."

The Counselor lifted his brows. "Diamonds . . . hereabouts?"

"The location can be verified once the claims are staked."

"How much capital does the Don need?"

"We expect to raise seven hundred fifty thousand to a million dollars."

"That is serious money."

"So is our mine property."

"I must say I've never heard of precious stones in North America, much less diamonds. It must be a most extraordinary find."

"It is. Can you raise the money?"

"What might I use to entice potential investors?"

The ferret reached in his coat pocket and drew out a glittering handful. "There is more where these came from."

"May I?" He held out his hand. The stones felt heavy. Legitimate to the touch.

"Can you raise the money?"

"I can find potential investors. Raising the money will likely require . . . more where these came from."

"Leave that to us. How long will it take?"

"I'll leave for San Francisco tomorrow. That should get us a start in two weeks' time. After that, we may find interest in New York. How do you wish for me to notify you?"

"Wire E. at this hotel."

"E.?"

"It is enough."

Endicott and his black manservant arrived at the U. P. Hotel with much ostentation and booked the finest suite in the hotel. Both noticed Escobar lurking about the lobby and dining room, but neither made acknowledgment or contact for more than a week. Contact, when it came, consisted of a note slipped under the door to the suite.

Counsel has arranged a meeting at Stanford House in San Francisco.
Proceed at once. He will contact you there.

E.

Stanford House
San Francisco

The carriage clattered up the hill over cobblestone paving to the digging clip-clop of a high-stepping chestnut gelding. The driver turned into a circular drive, approaching an imposing entryway dripping in elegance. A doorman, uniformed in dark green with brass buttons, opened the carriage door.

"Welcome to Stanford House," he said.

Endicott stepped down with a nod and started up the steps to the entry as though in a hurry and unimpressed by his surroundings. His man stepped down and hastened to follow along.

The arrogant bastard acts like he believes this little charade. Then the prospect of money represented by the heavy case he carried took over. Duval set his pique aside.

Inside, an expansive lobby gleamed of polished marble and teak. A rich oriental carpet created an island of color in the center of the room. An immense, polished, round table rose from the carpet, dominating the center of the room. A large floral display set in a tall porcelain vase graced the table top. Exotic flowers splashed vibrant color that played in the soft light of a heavy crystal chandelier suspended over the table from an arched ceiling two stories above.

Endicott scarcely noticed. He crossed the lobby on purposeful strides to the registration counter. "Your finest suite, please."

"Very good, Mr. . . ." The clerk spun the register.

"Endicott, Jeremiah Endicott."

"Yes, thank you, Mr. Endicott. We've been expecting you."

Endicott paused, pen in hand. He lifted a brow in query.

"We're holding this message for you."

He tore open the envelope. *Salon B.* He handed the note to Duval.

"Suite two-oh-one." The clerk passed the key across the counter.

"Have our bags taken up to the room. Where is Salon B?"

"A private room at the back of our main salon." He gestured to the lounge off the lobby. "Bell service!" He clapped.

Endicott tossed a gold eagle to the uniformed bellman and led the way to the lounge. A discreet plate lettered *Salon B* identified the door to a private salon with a small meeting table, fireplace, bar, and conversational groupings of velvet-upholstered Victorian furnishings. They were greeted by a tall, dark-eyed gentleman in a black frock coat.

"Mr. Endicott? Counsel at your service." He extended a hand and nodded to Duval. "You've arrived just in time. Our prospective investors should be here within the hour."

"Do you have a name, Counselor?"

He paused. "Kendrick will do. Do you have the stones?"

Duval lifted the leather case he carried.

"There on the table. Let's have a look at them."

He laid the case on the table, loosened the buckle strap fastenings, and opened the lid. Inside the velvet-lined case glittered with bright white diamonds salted with emeralds, rubies, and topaz.

"Magnificent," Counselor said. "Now close it. When our guests arrive, you'll both take your leads from me."

Duval smiled to himself as he closed the case. It looked like Endicott was about to get a taste of his own arrogance.

Forty-five minutes later they arrived. Counselor introduced the pair as Collis Crocker and Mark Leland. Leland was a prosperous railroad developer. Crocker parlayed right-of-way land speculation into a high-profile banking enterprise. Both men were turned out in fine style, wreaking of wealth. Counselor seated them around the table and proceeded to conduct the meeting.

"I've outlined the premise of your investment opportunity for these gentlemen. Our purpose here today is to confirm your claim and answer any questions they might have concerning the opportunity. Is that a fair summation?" He turned to the investors.

They nodded.

"Mr. Endicott, if you would then."

"As I'm sure Mr. Kendrick has advised you, I have discovered a strike rich in precious gems, diamonds primarily, with generous deposits of rubies, emeralds, and some topaz. Perhaps the best way to substantiate the claim is to show some of our initial findings." He opened the case and turned it to the investors, whose eyes went wide at the sight.

"Extraordinary!" Leland said.

Crocker held a large diamond up to the light. "Where is this claim of yours located?"

"That you must understand remains a closely guarded secret until all the arrangements and filings are in place," Counselor said.

"We will require expert verification of the find," the banker said, returning the diamond to the case.

"Of course," Endicott said.

"What led you to your discovery?" Leland asked.

"I have a university degree in geology and some mining background in working the Comstock Lode. My man here and I were on an exploratory expedition seeking silver deposits when we chanced upon geologic conditions conducive to the presence of gem formation. The stones you see before you are but a sampling of what we found."

"And you wish to syndicate your discovery," Leland said.

"Indeed. I lack the resources to develop the field even insofar as we've partially mapped it."

"How much do you expect you will require?" the banker asked.

"Six hundred to eight hundred thousand dollars should get us started."

"That seems a rather generous margin. Can't you be more precise?"

"As I said, Mr. Crocker, we've not yet fully mapped the field. That is our next step in development."

"I see. Of course, we will need a more precise figure, and, at that, it will take time to raise that sort of money. How do you plan to proceed?"

"My client is prepared to offer you gentlemen five percent interest in their mine for fifty thousand dollars. That will supply the funds to complete their survey and file a comprehensive claim," Counselor said.

The investors exchanged glances.

"Highly speculative." Crocker cautioned.

"Fully collateralized," Counselor said.

"Collateral?" The banker lifted a brow.

"There." Counselor nodded to the case.

"Ten percent," Leland said.

Counselor deferred to Endicott.

"Seven."

The investors exchanged glances.

"You hold the collateral, Collis. I'll draw a draft for twenty-five thousand on my account."

The banker turned to Kendrick. "It would appear we have a deal."

CHAPTER THIRTEEN

Stanford House

Bright sunlight spilled across the elegant setting in the Stanford House dining room. The midday lunch crowd customarily thin afforded Crocker and Malthus a quiet backdrop for an affable luncheon. The waiter in a starched, white jacket served an excellent seafood chowder and sherry.

"So what sort of larceny has the banking business got you up to these days?" Malthus said with a good-natured smile.

"Larceny, Montegue? Please. I have my reputation to consider."

"Ah, yes, ever the upright banker. Well then, how's business?"

"Banking is steady, much like insurance. We have our income mitigated by the occasional loss."

"Nice you have the perspective of income; my line seems focused strictly on losses."

"What are you working on now?"

"The International Import robbery."

"I read about that in the *Chronicle*. Rather substantial that one."

"It is, and not much more to go on than the morning fog when it lifts."

"At least we have one thing in common."

"What might that be, pray tell?"

"Jewels."

"The bank's taking gems on deposit?"

Crocker shook his head. "No, a rather intriguing investment opportunity Mark Leland and I recently bought into. You might find it interesting when it comes to the next round of syndication."

"What sort of investment?"

He glanced around the room conspiratorially. "A diamond mine."

"Here about?"

"West of the Rockies."

"That takes in quite a lot of territory."

"The exact location is a secret until the claim is fully mapped."

"And you've invested in this claim. Sounds speculative."

"Our initial investment is fully secured by the stones presented as proof of the claim. Further investment depends on verification of the field, following mapping and filing the claim. Interested?"

"Yes, I am but likely not for the reason you might imagine. I'd be interested in showing this collateral of yours to my client at International Imports."

"As an expert gemologist?"

"As a matter of coincidence."

"You think there might be a connection to his loss?"

"One never knows. I should think you would want to hear his view before putting additional capital at risk."

International Imports

High afternoon sun failed to improve either the atmosphere or décor in the Spartan facility. Crocker spread stones across a black velvet cloth on the cracked countertop. Furgeson examined them one by one under his jeweler's loupe. Malthus and Crocker waited expectantly, haloed in window glass before a curtain of dust motes. Furgeson pursed his lips and nodded.

"The stones are undoubtedly genuine."

Crocker smiled. Vindicated.

"Could they be part of your loss?" Malthus said.

The importer shrugged. "It's possible, but uncut, one can't be certain."

"But it is possible?"

"I suppose, but why do you suspect so?"

"Coincidence offends my sense of logic."

The importer shrugged. He turned to the banker. "Should the bank wish to sell them, I would be pleased to quote you a price."

"As of now, they collateralize a loan; but I shall take your generous offer under advisement should the need to liquidate the collateral arise."

"Liquidate being a euphemism for loan default," Malthus said.

The banker winced.

They thanked Furgeson and stepped outside.

"Before you go, Collis, might I have another question or two?"

"Of course."

"Who approached you with this diamond mine investment?"

"A lawyer from Chicago by the name of Kendrick initiated the contacts. He represents a gentleman by the name of Endicott who discovered the field."

"What can you tell me of Endicott?"

"Bright young fellow. Well cut. University educated in geology, which enabled him to recognize conditions favorable to the formation of precious stones. He has mining experience with Comstock."

"And he's the sole claimant?"

"No one else was represented. Just Endicott and his manservant."

"Manservant?"

"Big black chap. Bit of a French accent . . . I took for Cajun. Why all the suspicion, Monte?" He patted the case. "We've got stones good as gold here."

"As I said in there, coincidence offends me."

"Coincidence to you, rubbish to me."

Malthus shook his head as his friend strolled away.

Shady Grove

A racking cough cut short the Colonel's narrative. It passed.

"Have you seen a doctor for that?"

"Pill-pushing quacks? Hell no. I'm old. We're allowed our infirmities."

"It's only my genuine concern for your well-being."

"I'm touched. These stories, of course, have no part in that."

"Not really. Your weekly ration assures me of your continued interest." I eyed the bulge in his lap robe. "What happened next?"

"Malthus communicated his suspicions to me. It was only coincidence until he mentioned the Cajun. That sounded a curious note. It might never have amounted to more than that, had we not had the outbreak of jewel robberies that followed."

"Jewel robberies?"

"Time for supper, Colonel."

She'd come on us so quietly neither of us noticed. I smiled. She returned her Mona Lisa.

"It appears your jewel robberies will have to wait until next week, Robert. It seems I'm due for my next round of poison."

"Hardly poison, Colonel. Your complaining does absolutely no good."

"Oh, but you're wrong, my dear. It makes me feel better. As though I still have some sway over my circumstances. I don't, of course, but at least I have the freedom to delude myself. At my age, one must cling to the barest of things."

"See you at six, Robert."
She wheeled him away.

CHAPTER FOURTEEN

Cheyenne

Counselor cringed at the ferret's choice of a meeting place. The Red Lantern was a far cry from Stanford House. The sprawling two-story clapboard in the next block to the depot catered to train crews. The small yard and front walk were littered with lanterns alerting railroad officials as to the whereabouts of their crews should they be needed. He climbed the house steps and entered a shabby reception lounge, where he was greeted by a plump, painted blonde clad in scarlet undergarments with laudanum vacant eyes.

"I'm looking for *Señor* Escobar."

She pulled a pout and tossed stovepipe curls in the direction of a darkened hallway.

"Second door on the right."

From the hallway, the scent of cigar smoke would have given the ferret's presence away without benefit of directions. His knock elicited a muffled summons. Endicott and Duval were already there, seated around what must have been a card table in a sparsely furnished room. A bottle of tequila and glasses stood on the table. Escobar seemed to be the only one enjoying his choice of refreshments.

"You have the money?"

Counselor opened his case and stacked fifty thousand dollars in cash on the table. Escobar held out his hand for the case and repacked the currency.

"At fence prices, this purchases many stones for your mine," Escobar said. "Where will you locate it?"

"South in the foothills," Endicott said.

Escobar turned to Counselor. "And what of further investors?"

Counselor nodded. "I've had dealings with another in New York who has the appetite for such a venture. I leave on the morning train."

"Have you something with which to entice them?"

"We kept a small stake aside from the collateral."

"*Bueno.* How long do you expect to be in New York?"

"No more than a few days. I should be back in three weeks' time."

Escobar stubbed out his cigar. "Will you have your claim staked by then?"

Endicott nodded.

"Return to the hotel when you finish. Counselor will file your claim on his return from New York. I will meet you as soon as we have purchased the stones you will use to prepare your field. Once that is done, Counselor will invite the investors to verify the claim."

"We shall have to play that part carefully, depending on who the investors send," Counselor said.

"Leave that to me," Endicott said. "Unless they find an expert geologist I should be able to handle the inquiry. Even if they find a geologist we may be able to prevail. After all, the stones are there."

"See to it, *señor* geologist. Now you may leave one by one. I have another appointment."

The painted blonde waited in the hall as Counselor left. *Appointment indeed.* He recoiled inwardly at the unbidden thought.

Denver

Late afternoon turned the office sepia gold tinged in blue

foreshadows of evening. Kingsley's thoughts turned to prospects of a whiskey, dinner, and perhaps . . . yes, indeed, a visit with Madame Marie. The realization dawned—it had been awhile. Ah, the vitality of youth . . . where had it gone? These days he preferred a more tasteful experience. Taste and experience fit Marie Ambrochette. She'd be pleased to see him of course. At her stipend, she should be pleased. She seldom entertained personally any longer, but she made exception for "My Reggie," as she teasingly called him. Their mutual affections had blossomed to somewhat more than mere carnal gratification. They managed a degree of companionship unusual to the lady's profession. It helped perhaps that he retained her services on behalf of the firm as one of his vipers, though the street term for informant felt unseemly in her case given the nature of their arrangement. Still, the term served a practical purpose when justifying expense vouchers to the head office.

The visitor bell clanged in the outer office. He glanced at his pocket watch. Now what could be coming along at this hour? Trevane greeted the lad who delivered for Western Union.

"Telegram for Mr. Kingsley."

Trevane tossed the lad a quarter and headed for Kingsley's office. The managing director met him at the door.

"Now, what do you suppose this is all about on the cusp of evening?"

Trevane handed him the envelope. It had the aroma of head office all over it.

Urgent
Three jewelry store robberies reported in the past five days. St. Louis, Omaha, Cheyenne. Pattern seems headed your way. Be alert. Jeweler's Protective Union demands results.

"Anything special?" Trevane said.

"Jewel robberies. Three of them headed our way. Chicago has

their knickers in a knot over the client's expectations. It makes me wonder." He traced the crisp tips of his moustache along his lip with his fingers.

Trevane waited expectantly.

"It makes me wonder if our Cajun friend might be back in business."

"You don't suppose we could work another exchange."

"That might make too much to credit to coincidence. Pity though; it worked out so well the last time. Best we be on the lookout. He might have information useful to a more fulsome recovery."

Tiberius Brumble turned over the *Closed* sign and locked the front door. Traffic on the street slowed at day's end. He began the nightly ritual of emptying the display cases and securing the valuable merchandise in his safe. A smallish masked man with a big Walker revolver stepped out of the back workroom.

Brumble froze. "What do you want?"

The little fellow chuckled. "Guess." He threw the jeweler a gunnysack. "Fill it."

"How did you get in here? The back door was locked."

He laughed again. "Picking the lock was easier than blowing your safe. Now shut up and fill the sack."

Brumble emptied all three cases at the front of the store.

"Now the safe." The big gun waved to the back workroom.

Brumble grimaced, hoping the thief might have overlooked the unmounted stones stored there. With the safe cleaned out, the thief drew a chair to the center of the room. He tied the jeweler to the chair and gagged him. Satisfied no alarm would be raised anytime soon, he slipped out the back door to the ally and disappeared into the night.

Brumble arrived at our offices late of the day following the robbery. It had taken him most of the night to work himself free of his bindings. He notified the local police, who initiated their customary investigative procedures. A kindly inspector, one of ours actually, recognizing the likelihood the thief had already fled beyond their jurisdiction, suggested the jeweler contact the league. I summoned Cane and Longstreet to my office to hear the complaint. Brumble recounted the events of the previous evening.

"Is there anything more you can tell us of the thief?" Longstreet said. "Might he have had a scar or any other distinguishing feature?"

The jeweler thought for a moment, started to shake his head, and then paused. "Wait, there is one thing. I don't know if it will help. He was wearing a hat, but I'm pretty sure he had red hair."

"A short man with red hair." That's something to go on.

"I'd like to have a look at the store," Cane said.

"Good, then. Mr. Brumble, let me assure you the Great Western Detective League is on the case. Briscoe will visit your store in the morning. Beau, get the word out: we're looking for a short man with red hair."

The following morning, I accompanied Cane to Brumble Jewelers only to discover his Lordship Sir Reginald Kingsley and one of his agents preceded us there. I thought it odd until I recalled Montegue's suspicion.

"Well, well, Sir Reggie, what have we here?"

"I might ask the same, Crook. What brings you here?"

"Mr. Brumble here has engaged our services to recover his loss. And you?"

"The Jeweler's Protective Union is a Pinkerton client."

"Mr. Kingsley tells me there has been something of a rash of jewelry store robberies in recent days," Brumble said.

Kingsley scowled, displeased at the leak of useful information.

"A rash," I repeated. "So, Reggie, could it be the Cajun box man who recently slipped through your fingers with half of his ill-gotten gains is up to his old tricks again?"

"This was hardly the work of a box man. And before you get lordly over a perpetrator slipping through our fingers, may I remind you we recovered half of his proceeds, which is more than your so-called league has managed."

"It appears that worked out well, for both of you, doesn't it?"

"Both of us?"

"Pinkerton and the thief. You claim credit for a partial recovery, and the perpetrator avoids the inconvenience of incarceration."

"I resent the implication of that comment."

"No implication intended; merely an observation. Our reputation a little tender, is it?" I simply couldn't resist the opportunity to poke at his lordship's British sensibilities.

"Trevor, have you any further questions for Mr. Brumble?"

The tall, well-made young man shook his head.

"I don't believe I've met this young fellow. David Crook, Colonel, US Army retired, at your service." He took my hand.

"Trevor Trevane."

"And this is Briscoe Cane."

Cane and Trevane exchanged glances.

"Well then, Crook, we shall be toddling along. Important work to do and all that, you know."

"Perpetrators running free as we speak."

He stomped out in a huff. I made no effort to suppress a smile.

"What do you make of it?" Cane said on the walk back to the office.

"I can't shake the suspicion there might be a connection between the International Imports job and a sudden rash of jewelry store hold-ups. Is it possible Sir Reggie's pinch mucked up some larger scheme?"

"Anything's possible, but what sort of scheme?"

And there he had me. I had no idea, just this persistent gnawing in the gut that there was more here than coincidence. Fortunately, the irritant in my gut didn't disrupt my digestion long. We arrived at the office to find Longstreet anxiously awaiting our return.

"A man matching our boy's description bought a ticket on the Butterfield Stage two days ago."

"Bound for?"

"Santa Fe."

"You think it could be *El Anillo*?" Cane said.

"Another coincidence? That premise has started to unravel."

"You two are on your way to Santa Fe."

CHAPTER FIFTEEN

Shady Grove

All this talk of diamonds had yet to reveal any insight into my shopping dilemma. I visited Brumble Jewelers, now in the hands of the former proprietor's son, Joshua. He responded to my request to see wedding bands with the usual assortment of gold and silver circlets. When I asked his opinion of stones, he brightened. So did the prices. He assured me, as had his competitor, the stone was an investment. At the prices he quoted, you could be sure it was an investment, though I couldn't envision a circumstance where such an investment might be liquidated at a profit. Still I could only imagine the look in Penny's eye at the offering of such a handsome testament to our love. I left, pleading the chance to think it over on the walk to Shady Grove.

I was greeted in reception by news the Colonel had been somewhat indisposed of late. The nurse in reception would see if he was up to our usual visit. Penny came to reception in response to the query.

"He's quite insistent on meeting with you, Robert. I must warn you, though, he tires easily, suffering from his complaints. You can meet him in the solarium. He'll grouse about not going outside, but we can't allow him to risk a chill."

"Is his illness serious?"

She shrugged. "At his age, these things are not to be trifled with."

I repaired to the solarium. Presently Penny wheeled him in. He slouched noticeably in his chair.

"There you are, Robert. I thought you'd never get here."

"I'm sorry, Colonel." I wasn't late, but it was easier to indulge him.

"Well see you don't make a habit of it."

Penny slipped me a Mona Lisa behind his back and left the room. He waited to be sure she was gone before producing the empty bottle from beneath his lap robe.

"Do you think this is wise?"

He lifted a brow in question.

"I mean, considering your condition and all."

"Condition?" He coughed. "You sound like the quacks who infest this place. You provide the only beneficial medicinal therapy I receive."

He held out his hand for our weekly exchange. I set aside better judgment and handed over the bottle.

"Have you made any progress on your investment decision?"

"As a matter of fact, I've just come from Brumble Jewelers."

"Brumble . . . you mean they're still in business?"

"Tiberius's son Joshua manages the business now."

"Have you found an answer to your precious-stone question?"

"I've found alternatives to consider. You'll be sure to know when I reach a decision."

"I see. Now, where were we?"

I consulted my notes. "A man matching the suspect in the Brumble robbery purchased a stage ticket to Santa Fe. You'd dispatched Cane and Longstreet to pursue him."

"Ah yes." He closed his eyes.

Denver

Longstreet made an unusual midday arrival at the widow O'Rourke's, bounding up the stairs to his room. Maddie wiped her hands on her apron and followed him upstairs, where she found him packing a bag.

"And where might we be off to this time?"

"Santa Fe."

"The jewel case?"

He nodded over a clean shirt.

"Is Pinkerton on this case also?"

"They are. They've been retained by the Jeweler's Protective Union."

"Oh."

"Oh what?"

"Nothing. I seem to recall they were on the case the last time you ran off to Santa Fe."

"You've a good memory. I'd almost forgotten."

"I'm sure. Will that woman be in need of a room this time?"

Longstreet paused his packing, a self-satisfied gleam in his eye. "Samantha? Haven't seen hide nor hair of her since she went back to Chicago."

"You'd almost forgotten."

He turned to her where she stood in the door to his room. "Why Maddie O'Rourke, I do believe I detect a note of jealousy in your tone."

"Jealousy? Nonsense! Don't delude your detective self. I merely wondered if I needed to clean the spare room."

"Of course you did." He closed his case. "A little jealousy is good. It means you'll miss me properly whilst I'm gone. Just the thing to have a fella pining for his return to you."

"Properly pining? Do you think I've just fallen off the green grocer's cart?"

He started for the door. "Heavens no. I just know you'll miss me." He dropped his case and swept her up in a kiss.

She clenched a free fist and hit him on the shoulder. Once again with no conviction. Resistance melted. She surrendered to the moment.

He released her. "There. Now you can miss me proper."

"You are positively a rogue, Beau Longstreet."

He laughed. "But a lovable rogue." He picked up his case and bounded down the stairs.

She sank against the door frame, furious with . . . with unbidden discomfit.

CHAPTER SIXTEEN

New York

For all their past dealings, they'd never met before. Gould preferred it that way. The Counselor had proven useful when one of his business dealings or enterprises faced the need to cross to the other side of the law. Anonymity afforded a perfect break in any chain of evidence. He never would have agreed to meet the man had it not been for the extraordinary nature of the proposition he offered. They both understood this would, of necessity, be the final dealing in a long and profitable relationship.

Jay Gould made winning a habit. He did so by making his own rules. Conventional rules need not apply to the diminutive financier. He made enemies and detractors, mostly the victims of his schemes. He was a shadow to the law. A man removed from his deeds by cutouts, shell corporations, and a heavy veil of deniability. He was hated for it. One fellow speculator thought him wholly loathsome without redeeming humanity. Another characterized him as a "ruthless predator, Satanic in his manipulations." Gould found the venom flattering. He bested them, and they hated him for it. He thought it mildly amusing, but only mildly. The only thing that truly amused Jay Gould was money, lots of money. In this case, if the reliable Counselor were to be believed, diamonds and precious stones abounded in dazzling proportions.

The anticipated knock sounded at the office door. Gould

opened his desk drawer, drew out the .38 pocket pistol secreted there, and dropped it into his coat pocket. One never took precautions in hindsight. He crossed to the office door and admitted his caller.

"Pleasure to make your acquaintance, sir, after all these years." The man held out his hand. Gould ignored it.

"Have a seat."

Counselor followed him across the office. The little man all but disappeared behind a massive desk, swallowed up by a red leather chair.

"Now tell me about this mine you are trying to finance."

Counselor opened his case and spilled a small pile of stones on the desk. "These speak quite eloquently for themselves."

Gould hunched forward in his chair. He picked up a large diamond and held it up to the light. He tossed the stone back on the pile.

"Have you assessed the extent of the strike?"

"A complete mapping is underway, though preliminary reports suggest the field may span several miles."

"Has the claim been filed?"

"Not yet. We need to complete the mapping."

"So, the exact location is secret and not yet available for confirming inspection."

"Correct."

"How much are you seeking to raise to develop the field?"

"Eight hundred thousand."

Gould pursed his lips beneath a furrowed brow. "A goodly sum. Have you any commitments as yet?"

"San Francisco investors purchased seven percent for fifty thousand to finance mapping and filing the claim. On confirmation, they are prepared to come in for a full four hundred thousand."

"So, you're looking for another four hundred thousand."

He nodded.

"May I ask who the San Francisco investors are?"

"Collis Crocker and Mark Leland."

Gould drummed his fingers on the desk. "I'd like to verify these stones."

"How do you propose to do that?"

"I'm acquainted with an expert, one who might also be a prospective investor."

"Who might that be?"

"Charles Sterling."

"The jeweler?"

"The jeweler."

Counselor scooped the stones into his case.

Sterling & Co.

Opulent was the only way to describe the place, even for the Counselor, who was little impressed by such things. Glass, crystal, gold, silver, rich polished wood, china, ceramics— elegance everywhere you looked. The aquiline featured jeweler in frock coat and brocade vest sat at a small, velvet covered table, examining stone after stone through his loupe. He placed the last on his cloth.

"Remarkable, Jay."

"Authentic?"

"Quite. You say you have an opportunity to invest in developing the mine these came from?"

Gould nodded.

"I should think it a rare opportunity."

"The syndicate has preliminary commitments of four hundred thousand, pending confirmation and the claim filing. They are looking to raise an additional four hundred thousand. If a one hundred-thousand-dollar share were available, would it interest you, Charles?"

"Only one hundred thousand?"

Gould smiled. "I'll take that for a yes; and, yes, one hundred thousand only. There is a limit to my largess."

"I might have guessed."

Counselor declined Sterling's invitation to lunch with him and Gould. He left them with a promise to confirm the finding once the claim had been filed. He hailed a hansom cab and instructed the driver to take him to the train station. He settled into the seat as the cab lurched away and allowed himself a satisfied smile.

Securing a financing of such an amount was no small achievement. His share in the take would secure a comfortable future in pleasant surroundings where he could disappear without trace. The symmetry of concluding his relationship with Gould in such fashion amused him. How many mighty men had he assisted the little financier in besting? He'd taken the risks and survived by his wits. The arrogant little popinjay had taken the profits. True, he'd been paid well enough, but hardly a sum commensurate with his contributions. This time would be different. This time he'd take a profit while little Jay Gould got an unaccustomed comeuppance. He gazed out the carriage window as New York scrolled by. He permitted himself a soft chuckle. He'd best the best and disappear into the sunset.

CHAPTER SEVENTEEN

Santa Fe

The Denver & Santa Fe Stage clattered west on Washington taking right-of-way from pedestrian and sparse mounted traffic. It wheeled south on Palace and rolled to a stop at its station. Longstreet and Cane unfolded cramped limbs and climbed out. The driver and station master made quick work of unloading the coach boot, depositing their bags on the boardwalk. The station master directed them to the Capitol Plaza Hotel up the street the way they'd come in the next block west on Washington.

"So now all we have to do is find a little red-haired needle in this haystack," Longstreet said as he picked up his bag and started up the boardwalk toward the stately hotel.

"Chances are, we won't find him in the high rent district," Cane said.

"I feel a saloon case coming on."

"That'd be my guess."

They rounded the corner on Washington to the hotel grand entrance. A graciously appointed lobby turned out in dark wood greeted them. They checked into their rooms and set off canvassing saloons. Longstreet worked the sporting girls while Cane befriended bartenders. Afternoon had worn into early evening when they chanced on a seedy cantina on Grant Street. Longstreet caught the eye of a smoky working girl who became talkative for the price of his bottle of tequila.

"This friend of yours, you say he is *poco hombre con el pelo rojo*?"

"My Spanish ain't too good, darlin'.'' He stretched out a hand. "Little man with red hair." He picked red from her skirt.

She smiled with her eyes. "*Sí,* he has been here."

"Does he come here often?"

She nodded.

"In the evening?"

She glanced around the room, growing uncomfortable. "Why do you ask?"

"I owe him some money; I was hoping to repay."

"Sometimes. I say no more."

"Why?"

"Es dangerous. You want go upstairs?"

"Maybe some other time."

She went off in a huff.

Longstreet caught Cane's eye in the bar mirror. He jerked his head toward the door. Outside, night shadow settled over the street.

"He comes here sometimes. I say we set up a watch."

"Best lead we got for the moment."

"I'll take the alley across the street. There's a bench just down the block in front of that cigar store."

"I don't see it," Cane said.

"I know, but it's there. With luck, our boy won't see it, either."

They set up their watch. Two hours later a smallish fellow swung around the corner from Palace, making for the cantina on stubby legs. He disappeared inside. Cane followed him. Thirty minutes later a man of slight frame rounded the corner on Palace, following the little man's footsteps to the cantina. Something about the man registered a faint familiarity with Longstreet. He crossed the street to the boardwalk, fronting the cantina. He picked them out through the grime-steaked window at a back corner table. The little red-haired jewel thief and the ferret faced *El Anillo* man known as Escobar. It appeared they concluded their business rather quickly. Escobar disappeared into the dark reaches at the back of the smoky room.

Longstreet dashed down the alley to the back of the cantina. The adjoining alley stretched out black silence in both directions. He waited. Nothing. He turned to the cantina back door and drew his gun. He climbed the back step and tried the latch. The door opened. He stepped into a dark hallway. He paused to listen. A stairwell climbed to a dark upper floor. He made his way down the hall toward the lighted cantina.

The thief started at the sight of Longstreet, gun drawn. He scraped back his chair and turned to run straight into the muzzle of Cane's .44. Longstreet holstered his gun and drew handcuffs out of his coat pocket.

"What's goin' on here?"

"You're under arrest," Cane said.

Longstreet snapped his wrists behind his back.

"What's the charge?"

"Robbery."

"I ain't robbed nobody."

Longstreet frisked the man, drawing a .38 pocket pistol from one coat pocket and a bundle of new currency from another. "Looks like he already fenced the stones."

Cane glanced around the room, gun in hand, checking to see if the man had any friends in the place. Satisfied, he holstered his gun. "Bring him along. Let's see if the sheriff's got a cage to fit him for the night."

Upstairs, the smoky-eyed whore's door opened a crack. Ferret-like eyes peered out from the shadows as two familiar figures escorted the thief out of the saloon. The death warrants were signed. Now it was little more than the matter of serving them.

CHAPTER EIGHTEEN

Sheriff's Office

Cane and Longstreet arrived at the sheriff's office the following morning. They were shown into the cell block where their prisoner was being held. He sat on the bunk in a surly demeanor. They drew up chairs outside his cell.

"We've got a few questions," Cane said. "And all morning to get them answered before the afternoon stage to Denver. You're in a great deal of trouble."

"I don't know what you're talking about."

"Oh, I think you do. We're talking about the Brumble Jewelers heist in Denver. You arrived in Santa Fe a few days ago from Denver. You match the description of the robber and a man who bought a stage ticket for Santa Fe. We find you consorting with a known criminal and in possession of ten thousand dollars in cash. That's a lot of walkin' around money by anyone's standards. The kind of money a fence might pay for jewels valued at thirty thousand dollars. It would be wise if you cooperated. It might go easier on you."

"I still don't know what you're talkin' about."

Longstreet shook his head. "Not smart."

"What's your name?" Cane said.

No answer.

"Red will do for now. They'll give you a number when they lock you up . . . that is, if you make it to the lockup," Longstreet said.

"You threatening me?"

"Me? Never. It's just that the man you sold those jewels to is part of a crime syndicate, calls itself *El Anillo*. But you knew that, didn't you? Here's the thing: The Ring don't take kindly to birds like you who sing."

A visible shadow crossed his eyes even in the dimly lit cell. "I ain't sung nothin'."

"You know that, and I know that, but does *El Anillo* know that? They only know what we let them find out."

"That's murder."

"You know that. I don't know that. Now, if you were to co-operate, it'd be worth our while to keep our little secret. Lockup might be better for your health than anything your greasy little pal might come up with."

Silence. He shifted on a noisy bedspring.

"The name's Fellows. They do call me Red."

"That's better. You're not alone when it comes to jewel heists. We've seen something of a rash of them lately. Why?" Cane said.

He shrugged. "The word is out. *El Anillo* is buying."

"Why?"

"I don't know, and that's the truth, so help me."

"I expect it is."

Santa Fe Trail

The Denver stage rolled out of Santa Fe headed north. Cane sat beside the handcuffed prisoner. Longstreet sat across from Red, beside an attractive, dark-eyed woman noticeably uncomfortable in the presence of one of her traveling companions. She held a handkerchief over her nose to suppress the dust billowing off the team and coach wheels.

"Is he . . . dangerous?"

Longstreet gave his most attractive-woman-reassuring smile. "Not so long as we're here, ma'm."

"What did he do?"

"Jewel robbery."

"Was anyone hurt?"

"No ma'm. Beau Longstreet, Great Western Detective League." He offered a hand.

She accepted it. "Sarah. Sarah McBride."

"Pleased to meet you, Mrs. McBride."

"It's 'Miss.' " Her eyes relaxed over the kerchief.

"Even more pleased to make your acquaintance, Miss Mc-Bride."

She blushed. Cane rolled his eyes. The miles rolled by. Red dozed. Longstreet made light conversation with Sarah. They left Cane with little to distract his discomfort from the heat, dust, jounce, and roll of the ride.

The stage slowed into a grade, climbing a narrow draw, judging by the view through the isinglass. The coach motion swung into a curve, sliding Sarah into Beau.

"Whoa!" The driver hauled lines.

"Hands up!"

Cane and Longstreet exchanged glances and drew their guns.

"We're being held up?" Sarah gasped.

"You, *hombres* in the coach, throw out your guns and step down if you don' want to see the *señorita* hurt."

Longstreet cut his eyes to Cane. "This ain't no holdup."

Red smiled.

Sarah cringed in terror.

"Throw down your guns now!"

Cane held Longstreet's eyes with his gaze exchanging unspoken intent. He dropped his .44 out the window. Longstreet followed his lead.

The coach door opened beside Sarah. The masked *bandito* holding a gun offered his hand.

"May I assist the *señorita* down?"

She wrinkled her nose, ignoring the offered hand, and climbed down. The bandit stepped back, keeping her between himself and the coach.

"Now, the two of you." He waved his gun at Longstreet and Cane.

They obliged. Cane felt the bulge of the Forehand & Wadsworth Bull Dog at his back. His blades were within easy reach. Two bandits held the driver and shotgun messenger at gunpoint. He couldn't see a play that didn't put the woman in danger. The door on the other side of the coach opened.

"Come, *Señor* Red," someone said.

The thief jumped down. "What about these?" He held up his cuffed hands. "The big one's got the key."

"We will take care of that soon enough. Come now, we must hurry."

The bandit shoved him to the front of the coach, where two horses waited.

Cold realization clutched at Fellows's chest.

"Now you two." The man shielded by Sarah waved Longstreet and Cane forward with his gun.

Longstreet glanced at Cane. He started as ordered. As he passed Sarah, he pulled her to the ground. Cane's boot blade stuck the nearest bandit in the throat. The Forehand & Wadsworth spit muzzle flash. The nearest mounted bandit toppled out of the saddle. Longstreet shoved Sarah under the coach and came up with his pistol.

The bandit behind Red fired. The prisoner's chest opened in a gaping exit wound.

The shotgun messenger dispatched the other mounted bandit with a savage eight-gauge blast.

The last bandit swung into the saddle of a flashy gold stallion and wheeled away, trailing covering fire. He disappeared around the bend in a cloud of dust.

Longstreet put an arm around Sarah, shaken near to swoon. He helped her up.

"It's over."

She leaned against him trembling. "I was never so scared in all my life."

"I'm sorry we had to put you in danger. They meant to kill us all."

"They did," Cane said.

"But why?" Sarah said.

"Witnesses," Cane said.

Escobar waited at an abandoned mine a mile west of the stage road. A single rider rode in and stepped down.

"What happened?"

"Gringos muy peligrosos."

"Where are the rest of your men?"

"Dead."

"Four men to two and three are dead?"

"Four men to three. The shotgun messenger got one of ours."

"And the red-haired thief?"

"I killed him."

Escobar clenched his teeth on a muffled oath.

"Should I raise some men and go after them?"

"And lose more good men? Don't be a fool. The little thief is dead. They know nothing. With luck, *Patrón* will not have you shot for stupidity."

CHAPTER NINETEEN

Colorado Foothills

A day's ride south of Cheyenne, Endicott drew a halt in gently sloping hill country. Here, early spring had beaten back the last vestiges of winter still clinging to the gray shrouded peaks at higher elevations. Wildflowers danced on the breeze beside white running streams under a dazzling midday sky running fluffy puffball clouds up the peaks to the east.

"I don't know about you, but I've had enough of tramping the wilds," Endicott said. "This looks like a diamond field to me. How about you?"

"You're the geologist."

Endicott smiled. "That's right, I am. Let's set a few markers to give the place the look of a claim. That'll make it easier to find when we come back with the stones."

They had the bogus claim marked out by evening. After a trail-fare supper, they settled into the snap and pop of a campfire beneath a blanket of twinkling stars spread to mock the soon-to-be-seasoned diamond field. An owl hooted in the distance. A coyote howled to its mate. Crickets sang melody over the harmony of creek burble. Duval produced a bottle from his saddlebags.

"Care to sweeten your coffee?"

"Don't mind if I do."

He splashed both cups.

"What's next?"

Endicott shrugged. "We've got a claim to file. The only other thing we might do is give the place a name."

"Once we get done with our planting we'll have us a Jeweled Garden."

Endicott laughed. "We will indeed. I had no idea you possessed the soul of a poet. 'Jeweled Garden' it is."

"Now that we've given poetic license to larceny, what's next?"

"We go back to Cheyenne in the morning and wait for Counselor to file our claim and the Don to deliver some bait."

"I was afraid that's what you'd say. I'm not good at waiting."

"Well, don't occupy yourself by blowing a safe. The last thing we need is that kind of heat this close to the prize."

Cheyenne
Three days later

Things got quiet away from the depot and red-light district in the small hours of the night. Duval window-shopped the jeweler that afternoon. He couldn't believe his good fortune. He slipped into an alley two doors down and made his way to the back of the shop. He inserted his pick in the lock and disappeared inside. Ambient starlight from the storefront windows colored the darkness. Just enough light to make out the safe behind the counter. He tried the handle and was rewarded with the confirmation he expected. This jeweler had yet to conceive of a man of his talents. He lent his ear to the lock and let his pick find its way home.

Click

The safe opened.

As he swept the contents into a case, one stone stood out even in low light. He held it up to catch the window glow. He'd never seen a diamond so large. He smiled Cheshire satisfaction. No sense burying this one in the ground. He knew precisely where to place it in return for a bounty of favors. He slipped the stone into his pocket and closed the case. He debated the humor of relocking the safe, deciding against spending needless time at the scene. He slipped into the alley and disappeared into the night.

Santa Fe Trail

With Longstreet occupied by Sarah and no prisoner to occupy him, Cane got some sleep on the return trip to Denver, half dozing through the rock and sway of the coach and some of the conversation.

"What brings you to Denver?" Longstreet said.

"I hope to find work."

"What sort of work?"

"I've experience as a bank teller."

"We definitely have banks. Do you have family there?"

She shook her head.

"Where will you stay then?"

"Hotel I suppose, until I find something more permanent."

Cane roused himself. "Widow O'Rourke's boarding house sounds like just the place, don't you think, Beau?"

Longstreet put a good face on an inward grimace. Cane might think it good sport. He could almost hear Maddie now.

"A widow's boarding house sounds perfect."

"I maintain a room there."

"Splendid! Then I should know someone in the bargain." She favored him with a sunny smile. "Do you suppose she might have a room available?"

"She might." *Of course she did. Samantha's no less.* His gut winced again.

"You'd best introduce Sarah to the widow when we arrive," Cane said. "No sense having her waste good money on an expensive hotel." Cane closed his eyes. His work finished.

"No sense," Longstreet said resignedly. No good would come of this, and he couldn't see a graceful way out. Cane would pay for this. He had no notion how or when, but he would . . . pay.

Sarah took his arm.

Denver

"What a lovely house," Sarah said, turning up the walk from the quiet, tree-lined street to the widow O'Rourke's boarding house.

Longstreet's mind raced. *How was he going to explain this? Somehow the truth seemed rather flimsy cover in this case. What possessed Cane to suggest such an arrangement? This of course. The predicament undoubtedly amused the old scoundrel.* He inserted his key in the lock. The familiar and welcoming scents of baking bread and wood polish shrieked unfamiliar foreboding.

"Hello." He hoped the greeting sounded casual.

Maddie poked her head out of the kitchen. Flour smeared her cheek. Her eyes flicked from Sarah to Longstreet.

"What have we here?"

"Maddie O'Rourke, may I present Sarah McBride."

Maddie crossed the dining room, wiping her hands on her apron. Her lips smiled. Her eyes were not amused. *Now what have we got up to here?*

"Sarah's just arrived in Denver. She's in need of a room. Briscoe suggested you might have one." The explanation came out too fast. It sounded a bit forced. It was.

"Briscoe, is it. Nice to meet you, Miss McBride. It is 'Miss,' isn't it?"

"Why, yes. Nice to meet you, too, Mrs. O'Rourke."

"Did you come in on the Santa Fe stage with Beau here?"

"I did. And fortunate I was to have him and Mr. Cane to save me from those horrible stage robbers."

"He does know his way around trouble. What happened?"

The question had an Irish edge. "We think *El Anillo* tried to liberate our prisoner."

"I see. How fortunate for Miss McBride to have had you

there in her time of need."

Sarah puzzled at the tone. "Have you a room then, Mrs. O'Rourke?"

"I'm afraid not, my dear."

Longstreet clenched the drop in his jaw.

"Pity, you have such a lovely home here. Would you know of any other respectable residences I might try?"

"I'm sorry, my dear, I don't. Might you, Beau?"

"At the moment, I can only suggest the Palace."

"Well, thank you both for your kindness. I can find my way back to the station."

"Good day, Miss McBride."

Longstreet watched her go. "You do have a vacant room."

"Of course."

"Then why not . . . ?"

"I'll not have that go on under my very nose."

"That? What 'that'?"

"You know perfectly well what that."

"Oh, that that."

"Yes, that that."

"There ain't no that to go on."

"Not in this house."

"Of that we can be sure," Beau said.

"We can," Maddie said.

"You know this conversation makes absolutely no sense . . . unless—"

"Unless what?"

"Unless . . . you know."

"I don't know."

"I think you do."

"I've no idea what you are talking about, Beau Longstreet."

"Unless you're jealous."

"Jealous? Nothing could be further from the truth."

"Oh? I don't know."

"Well, I do."

"I'm pleased to hear that. You know you're lovely with that flour smear on your cheek."

"Rrrgh!" She wiped her cheek with the back of a fist.

"Other cheek."

She turned on her heel.

"Missed me, too."

She stomped back to the kitchen.

CHAPTER TWENTY

Cheyenne

Duval turned up his nose as the Red Lantern front door creaked open. It wasn't that he had scruples when it came to frequenting brothels; it was merely a matter of taste. He much preferred those catering to a clientele of more refined tastes. The Red Lantern came with a tawdry powdered appeal scented in cheap perfume, equally cheap whiskey, stale tobacco smoke, and touches of oil and coal dust dragged in by the railroad crewmen who frequented the place. He arrived early to transact a bit of business with the Don's man before Endicott and the Counselor arrived. The dove in reception eyed him hungrily. *It must be the suit.*

"What can I do for you, sugar?" She fingered a lapel.

"I'm here to see *Señor* Escobar."

She pouted. "I believe *Señor* Escobar is . . . occupied at the moment. If you'd care to be occupied, I'm sure he'll be ready to see you when you are ready to see him." She smiled, revealing stained buck teeth.

"Tell him Duval is here."

She turned in a huff. He followed her down the darkened hall, leading away from reception. She knocked on the third door.

"Duval is here."

"He's early."

Duval spoke up over the whore's shoulder. "I've some business to discuss, if you're still buying."

"Show him into the card room. I'll be along directly."

"This way."

He followed her hips down the hall to the room where they last met. She opened the door and returned to reception. Moments later Escobar, clad in his britches, stepped in.

"What have you got?"

Duval drew a sack from his case and spilled the take from his heist on the game table.

"Cheyenne?"

Duval nodded.

"I heard. Too much heat so close to the operation."

"I don't see any heat."

"Eight thousand."

Duval laughed. "Twelve."

"Ten, but only because I need to finish a little something *es* already started."

Endicott and the Counselor arrived within minutes of one another.

"Where is Escobar?" Counselor said.

"He's finishing a little something. He'll be along directly."

"I can only imagine in such a splendid establishment," Counselor said.

Duval nodded assent. *At least the lawyer had taste.*

Escobar entered trailing a veil of cigar smoke. "Sit." He gestured to the table. He set two sacks of stones on the table. "These should cover the Don's investment."

Endicott opened one bag and examined the contents.

"Did you secure New York investors?" the ferret asked.

"We are fully subscribed at four hundred thousand, pending verification of the field."

"*Bueno.* You have the markings of the claim?"

106

Endicott slid a sheet of paper across the table. Escobar examined it and passed it to Counselor.

"File it." He pushed the sacks of stones to Endicott and Duval. "Deposit our claim. Continue on to Denver and await instructions at the Palace." He turned to Counselor. "When the claim is properly filed, see to the verification needs of our San Francisco investors. What will the New York investors require?"

"They will go along with the findings for San Francisco."

"*Bueno.* Then we need only pass the one inspection. When their requirements are complete, send me word here."

Counselor nodded.

What's the ferret got in that room to make him so partial to this dump?

Jeweled Garden

They'd staked the claim in a pie shape running north to south up the face of a rocky slope with a stream winding along the western boundary and a loose shale field up the east slope. Endicott and Duval made their base camp on the north end of the claim at the base of the slope. The following morning, they began salting the field. Endicott handed Duval a small sack of stones.

"These can go along the creek bed and banks. They should be easy to find when our investor comes along. Spread them out. These things don't grow in bunches."

Duval set off along the creek bank in the gray light of dawn. Endicott climbed the west slope above the creek to a prominent black rock outcropping. He knelt, drew a knife, and scraped a shallow furrow along the base of the rock. He seeded it with a few stones and covered them up. He climbed the slope, choosing distinctive formations and repeating the process. They continued their work through the morning, returning to base camp at midday.

Settled around a small campfire with a fresh pot of coffee, Endicott studied the east face of the slope. "We need to stay away from the shale."

"Why?" Duval asked.

"We don't just need to find these things; we need a geologically plausible story explaining why we found the field as we did. Stones are formed by the pressure of hard rock formations. You won't find them in soft stone shale."

"Sure you will, if we put them there."

"That's not the point. The point is we have a geologically plausible explanation for having found them where we did."

"We did?"

"Of course not; but the story is much more believable if we do. This afternoon we'll salt the eastern face of the slope. We won't need as many stones there. We'll discover a few to confirm the extent of the field. We'll bury them around the base of those black rock formations the way I did on the west face. We should finish up in time to ride on to Denver in the morning."

They worked their way up the central face of the slope, crossing over to the east slope in late afternoon. Heat built in as the day progressed. Both men glistened with sweat from their exertions.

"Planting these stones is near as much work as mining them," Duval said.

"Near enough."

A low grunt sounded in the undergrowth up the slope. Duval cut his eyes to Endicott. The geologist froze. He pressed a finger to his lips and reached for his gun. Bushes shook with the movement of a dark shape. Duval reached for his gun. The grizzly rose on her hind legs and bared dripping fangs and claws with a growl to roil a man's guts. Duval took aim.

"Wait!" Endicott hissed.

She squatted, alert to their presence. If she decided to charge downhill, she'd be on them in seconds. Moments passed. She gave a snort and lumbered off toward the creek, two tumbling bundles of cub trailing behind. Both men let out a breath.

"Why didn't you let me shoot her?" Duval said.

"Two reasons. Chances are you wouldn't have killed her with a hand gun. Wounded she'd only be more dangerous than she already is. You don't want any part of a sow with cubs let alone an enraged sow with cubs. Second, we've laid a small fortune in jewels out here. Grizz are territorial. She'll keep watch over our little garden after we pull out in the morning."

CHAPTER TWENTY-ONE

Denver
Pinkerton Office

Kingsley scowled at the telegram. Trevane paused at the office door.

"Something the matter?"

"Another jewelry store. Cheyenne this time. Jeweler's Protective Union has Chicago wound tighter than the curls on a House of Lords wig. They want results. I wonder about this one, though."

"How so?"

"Quite an accomplished burglar. No forced entry. Cleaned out a locked safe with no messy explosives. First-class box job."

"A professional job makes you wonder?"

"It does. It makes me wonder if our Cajun friend might be back in business."

"What do you think we should do?"

"If I'm right, it's time to give Chicago a result."

"You want me to head up to Cheyenne and have a look around?"

"Can't see him staying around after a job like that. It would appear *El Anillo* is still buying. Let's check our local sources here before we run off to Santa Fe."

"After what happened to the Weasel, street talk on The Ring has gone quiet."

"There is that. This time we know who we're looking for, and he's not *El Anillo.* Double the usual spiff. See if that might loosen a tongue."

Denver

Palace Hotel

The Palace dining room glittered in low light reflected in crystal, silver, fine china, and flowers set off against fine white table linen. The maitre d' showed Longstreet and Maddie to a candlelit corner table. Longstreet scarcely noticed the two gentlemen seated at an adjacent table. Maddie looked lovely. Something about a red-haired woman in a green gown. It turned her eyes to dewy emeralds and her complexion peaches and cream with just a pinch of cinnamon freckle. He'd persuaded her to forgive him for the awkward introduction of Sarah McBride, finally, it seemed, convincing her it was Cane's doing in hope of provoking the very reaction she'd visited on him. No woman can abide being so manipulated by a man. In the end, she'd dispensed forgiveness and accepted his offer of dinner. He couldn't be sure if she truly blamed Cane or simply gave up to the satisfaction of having extracted sufficient discomfort at his expense. He held her chair and took his seat. She busied herself with the menu. He absorbed the vision.

"And what, pray tell, might you be gawking at?"

"The loveliest woman in the room."

She rolled her eyes. "I agreed to accompany you to dinner. Your silver-tongued flattery is not required."

"You are an exasperating woman, you know. You simply cannot abide the notion a man might find you so . . . attractive."

"Sinfully attractive you mean. It's the sinful part that worries me."

"I assure you, Mrs. O'Rourke, I've only the most honorable of intentions."

"Honorable intentions, is it? That silver tongue of yours leads to a wee more licentious intention by my lights."

"I'm shocked you could so misestimate me."

"You're shocked. I'm shocked you think me so naïve."

"If you trust me so little, why ever do you put up with my attentions?"

A hint of a smile tugged at the corners of her mouth. "You amuse me."

A waiter in starched white jacket appeared. "Have you made your selections?"

"I'm afraid we shall need a few moments. One of us has yet to look at his menu."

"May I offer you an aperitif then?"

"Irish whiskey for me," Longstreet said with a smile.

"Make it two."

"There's a good lass."

"Lass is it now? You may not be of the old sod, Beau Longstreet, but a bit of the blarney has rubbed itself off on ye somewhere in your checkered past."

The waiter went off to fetch their drinks. Longstreet opened the menu. That's when it hit him. Unmistakable accent tinted in French. One of the men at the next table. He honed in on the conversation. Something about a mining claim. Geologic conditions made right for the formation of stones. Stones? Geology was stones.

The waiter returned with their drinks. "May I take your order?"

"I believe I'll have the shepherd's pie," Maddie said. "All this talk of home has me hungry for it."

Longstreet's attention returned to his table. "Ah, I'll have the special."

"I'm sorry sir, we don't have a special this evening."

"Oh, make it a steak then."

"Very good, sir."

"Thought long and hard over that one, did we?"

"Sorry, I was distracted."

"And there it is. One minute I'm the most fascinating creature alive and the next you're gone off to distraction."

Longstreet leaned forward. "Those men at the next table. What can you tell me about them?"

Her eyes drifted over his shoulder. "The tall one is a handsome devil. Might make for more interesting dinner conversation than present company. The big black man has a bit of a French accent."

"Cajun."

"How do you know?"

"He may play a part in an investigation we're working on. In fact, they both may."

"Have I stumbled into one of your investigations?"

"I believe you have."

"Oh, dear. Is it dangerous?"

"Could be. Are you armed?"

"Heavens no. Are you?"

"Of course. Now all we need to do is act natural."

"Natural?"

"Two lovers out for a pleasant evening together."

Her eyes shot wide.

Longstreet lifted his glass. "To us."

She lifted her glass, touching her rim to his. "How natural is natural?"

"Until you're amused."

Shady Grove

The Colonel nodded. Gray light creeping across the polished solarium floor whispered our time was coming to an end. He seemed tired. Strangely we had not completed the exchange of his weekly contraband, an act that by custom he concluded the moment Penny left us. He woke with a start.

"Sorry, Robert. I seem to have nodded off there for a moment."

"No trouble. It gave me a chance to organize my notes." I glanced at the door. "Penny may be along any time now. Do you have something for me?"

He shook his head. "Didn't finish. Maybe next week. Now, where were we?"

"Longstreet overheard Duval and Endicott in the Palace dining room."

"Ah, yes. We took it up with Cane the next morning. We were all taken with the highly suspicious circumstances of a suspect jewel thief discussing the claim of a diamond mine. It struck us as the sort of gambit to bring *El Anillo* out of the shadows. We discerned the pair were registered guests of the hotel, where upon I immediately ordered surveillance." He lapsed into a fit of coughing.

"Time for supper, Colonel." She smiled that little smile that captivated me so.

"And thus marks the passing of my days. One culinary delight followed by the next. Let's see, second Saturday of the month . . . that would be creamed beef on toast. They favor soft mush so as not to trouble us with the need of chewing."

"And he's wasting away for it," Penny said.

"Until next week, Robert."

I watched her wheel him away. A glitter of precious stone danced in my head.

We took in an early concert at the band shell in the park. It was a pleasant evening featuring a lively selection of contemporary favorites and old standards performed by the Denver City Orchestra Society, an amateur group whose performances were free. Later, over caramel and hot fudge sundaes at our favorite ice cream parlor, I broached the subject.

"How is he?"

She picked at her ice cream, eyes clouded with concern.

"He doesn't seem himself." I didn't dare say the cause of my concern.

"The cough wearies him. He sleeps more these days."

"Can nothing be done for the cough?"

"The doctor speculates as to its cause. It doesn't respond to treatment. And then, of course, there is his age. Nature's way takes its course in spite of our wishes."

I didn't like the sound of that. I suppose I considered the old curmudgeon timeless. My Penny reminded me time passes. I resolved to get on with our lives, whether in stone or band.

CHAPTER TWENTY-TWO

Velvet Ribbon

The street meandered quietly through blue-gray shadows into early evening. Here and there a gas light pricked the darkness. The stately Victorian bore a tasteful dignity not usually associated with establishments of her repute. A bow of lavender velvet ribbon tied about the whitewashed door post offered the only suggestion of the more provocative delights within. He climbed the broad front porch to the massive center entrance. He tapped a polished brass knocker. The door swung open to a waxed wood foyer lit by the large cut-crystal chandelier he remembered from his earlier visit. A stunningly attractive woman dressed in a lavender satin gown greeted him.

"Ah, Monsieur Duval, welcome back to our humble retreat." She closed the door behind him with a slight bow. "How may we be of service this evening?"

"I am surprised you remember my earlier visit, Madam Ambrochette."

"You are too modest, *monsieur*. One could hardly overlook a man of such refined sensibilities."

He smiled. "On my last visit, I was served by a most exquisite young lady; Carmel, I believe she said her name was."

"Ah yes, Carmel. Castilian you know."

"I did not. As you may recall, I was pressed by business that evening and had no time to properly make her acquaintance. If it please, I should like to rectify that."

"Oh, I'm sure Miss Saville would be most pleased to make your acquaintance. Right this way." She led him past a large parlor rendered elegant where the ladies of the Velvet Ribbon lounged in all their splendor. A warm paneled corridor, candlelit by wall sconces, passed rows of matching wood doors to the one she opened for him.

"Carmel will be along momentarily."

The room was candlelit. A massive four-poster bed dominated one side. A settee and wing chairs, upholstered in dark blue this time, clustered around a low table festooned with a vase of fresh flowers before a cheery fireplace, snapping and popping quietly against the spring evening chill. A lovely oriental rug completed the elegant comforts. The door had no more than closed when a soft rap sounded.

"Come in."

She smiled. Dark hair, dark eyes, skin the color of creamed coffee, dressed in a tastefully provocative gown. She carried a bottle of sherry and two glasses. She set the glasses on the table and poured. She handed him a glass; her eyes simmered smokily. She offered her glass in toast. A fine nutty burn warmed the room.

"There, that is much better. Now let us see to your comfort." She tugged his ribbon tie loose, took his glass, and slipped his coat off his shoulders. She handed him his glass. "Sit here." She patted the settee. She folded his coat over the back of a wing chair and sat on the settee, her back to him. Her fingers groped for the hooks fastening her dress. He set his glass aside, his fingers fumbling at the small hooks.

Cracking a safe came more easily.

"Ah, *sí*." She sighed, wriggled out of her dress, and tossed it across the chair. She collected her glass and settled beside him. Soft golden warmth clothed in a gauzy, ribbon-festooned chemise, the top two buttons shamelessly undone.

"What would *monsieur* care for?" Her voice soft and thick.

"I believe we are off to a fine start." He lifted his glass.

She dipped her finger in sherry and traced his lips. A mischievous glint turned sultry soft.

Ah yes, a fine start.

Longstreet leaned against an old oak, hidden in its shadow across the street and down the block from the Velvet Ribbon. He glanced at his watch as the evening wore on. *Expensive taste and stamina, too.* Well, we know where this one is for the night. *Time to go home to Maddie.* He caught himself thinking, *home to Maddie.*

Duval lifted a lid awake. She sprawled across the tempest-tossed four-poster, tangled in sheet, her hair a mass of dark curls. Magnificent. He'd had no better in New Orleans. He slipped out of bed and crossed the dimly lit dawn, collecting his discarded clothing. Money seemed so pedestrian at the moment. He'd kept the large diamond for a reason. He fished it out of his coat pocket and padded back to the bedside. Her hand caught his as he bent to place it on the nightstand.

"What is this?"

"For you."

Her eyes went round in the feeble light. "*Señor* is too generous."

"*Señorita* is too . . ." He groped for the word.

"Grateful?" She lifted the sheet and beckoned.

Velvet Ribbon
Two Days Later

Kingsley lounged on a settee covered in velvet of a royal purple. It suited her style. Marie Ambrochette was an exotic experience. She'd captivated him with wit, wisdom, and charm. Oh, yes, those charms. She owned the Velvet Ribbon. Ran it with an iron fist. All but retired from the trade personally, she indulged her Reggie for his cultured ways and an intellect she measured up to her own.

The door opened. She never knocked. She swept in to the room in a cloud of lavender satin, scented to match. Her chestnut tresses bound up in curls with ribbons of the same hue. She smiled even white, her lips a delicious crimson.

"I've a vintage cognac to christen our evening." She toddled along to the sideboard and poured. Her eyes brimmed anticipation as she brought drinks in cut crystal to the settee.

Never shy of ostentation, Kingsley noticed it at once. A spectacular, large diamond nestled in the cleft of her bosom, bound by yet another lavender ribbon. She handed him his glass and took her place beside him.

"I say, I don't recall seeing that bauble before. May I?"

"What, and begin before we've enjoyed our cognac and company?" she teased.

He lifted the stone from her breast, turning it to the light. "Magnificent."

"They still are, aren't they?"

"Of course, my dear. The stone, too." He smiled, returning it to its proper place with a playful back-of-the-hand caress.

"There, that's more to my taste, you nasty boy."

"Wherever did you get it?"

"A gentleman doesn't ask a lady such things."

"I am a nasty boy; you said so yourself."

"So I did. Rather fondly, too, I might add. Very well then, one of my most accommodating girls received it from a most appreciative client. I fancied the 'bauble,' as you term it. She fancied cash. I obtained it at a most agreeable price."

"Does this appreciative client have a name?"

"Reggie, dear, you know our policy. Absolute discretion. You of all people should understand and appreciate that."

"I have a professional interest. Was this client a black Cajun perchance?"

Her eyes spoke all the answer he needed.

"You are so very clever." She drained her glass. "There, that's spiked my appetite. Shall we begin?"

"I thought you'd never ask."

"Leave the diamond," she breathed.

Pinkerton Office

Trevane returned to the office the following afternoon and made straight for Kingsley's office. He filled the door frame, drawing Kingsley up from his most recent expense voucher.

"Found him."

"That didn't take long. Where?"

"He's registered at the Palace. The clerk believes he's in the employ of a man named Endicott. He suggests Duval is Endicott's gentleman's gentleman."

"Nothing about our boy suggests he would devote himself to anything like that. Not when he's handing out diamonds the size of walnuts in return for ladies' favors."

"Maybe the diamond is a fake."

"I doubt it. Even so . . ." He drummed his fingers on the desk. "No, I suspect the gentleman's gentleman ruse is the fake. But why?"

"There's more. We're not the only investigators interested in certain guests at the Palace."

"Oh?"

"I spotted Crook's man Cane, keeping an eye on things."

"Do you suppose they are on the lookout for someone else?"

"That would make for a great deal of coincidence."

"True. Then we shall keep our eyes on both of them."

"It would be nice to know what Crook's got."

"It would, wouldn't it. I believe I know how that might be arranged."

He scribbled a note and handed it to Trevane.
"Run this over to Western Union, and send it off to Chicago."
Trevane read the missive on the way to Western Union.

Possible break in the jewel robbery case.
Need agent Maples in Denver posthaste.

Kingsley

Now what could that possibly be about?

CHAPTER TWENTY-THREE

Pinkerton Office
Denver

Trevane glanced up at the sound of the outer office door. He arched a brow in surprise. *What have we here?*

She stepped out of the sunshine beyond the office door. Trevane rose to greet her. "Trevor Trevane, Pinkerton . . . may I be of assistance?"

She sized him up with a violet eye. *Perhaps.* She extended a hand.

"Samantha Maples. I'm here to see Kingsley. He still in there?" She lifted her chin to his office door.

"You're agent Maples?"

She savored the effect she had on the unsuspecting. "It would seem so. Is he in?"

"Samantha, we've been expecting you." Kingsley beamed. "Come in, come in."

She brushed past an incredulous Trevane into Kingsley's office. Agent Maples was a dark-eyed beauty with blue-black hair and a figure fit for a fairy-tale princess. She was about the last thing he'd expected.

"Come along, too, Trevor. You may be able to fill in some of Samantha's questions." He dropped his voice. "If you put your tongue back in your mouth, that is." He followed Trevane into the office and closed the door.

"So, what have we got?" Samantha said. "Chicago was pretty

terse. Possible breakthrough in the Jeweler's Protective Union case was about the sum of it."

"Indeed. We have a known jewel thief posing as a gentleman's gentleman for a chap representing himself to be a geologist."

"You have them under surveillance?"

"Oh, they are quite well surveilled. Actually, that's where you come in."

"I don't understand."

"We are not the only detection service watching the pair."

A wry smile pecked at her lips. "Beau Longstreet."

"Very perceptive. We thought you might renew your . . . acquaintanceship. See what they've got, if you will."

"I don't know. Beau and I left things a bit . . . shall we say, unsettled. Do we have anything to exchange?"

"We'd have to give that some thought. Of course, I wouldn't want you to do anything you find disagreeable."

"My exchanges with Longstreet have all been most agreeable; but we need to give him something."

"Trevor, what do you suggest?"

"It's a bit of a throw-away after all that's gone on. If they read the news accounts of the killing they've probably surmised the Weasel was an *El Anillo* job. We could confirm that and give up the fact he was one of our informants."

"Ah, very good. Juicy, but nothing really new to go on."

Samantha bit her lip prettily. "That might work. As I recall he left Pinkerton over a one-sided exchange with Crook's organization. He might be a trifle suspicious."

"Unavoidable, that one. I'm sure money was involved in his decision to leave our employ. Besides, I can't imagine him letting a little thing like suspicion get in his way with you."

Trevane glanced from Kingsley to Samantha, fighting the feeling he had no idea what was going on here.

"We'll go with the information on the Weasel," Kingsley said.

"How do you want to proceed?"

"I'll invite him to have drinks as a start."

"I can arrange for a messenger to run your invitation over to their office."

"Office?" She shook her head. "Too professional. Let's unsettle Beau a little. You get the messenger; I'll compose the note."

Kingsley and Trevane exchanged glances.

"Do as she says, Trevor."

O'Rourke House

Longstreet inserted his key in the door and stepped into the freshly polished foyer. Pleasant cooking aromas mingled with lemons and floor wax led to the kitchen.

"Something smells good."

She glanced over her shoulder, never leaving the chicken she was browning on the stove. "A message arrived for you this afternoon. It's on the dining table at your place. Interesting hand."

Frosty? What's that about? The envelope was addressed in a somewhat familiar feminine hand. He tore it open.

> *Drinks at the Palace? Shall we say six?*
>
> *Samantha*

"Something important?"

More accusation than question. "It may be a break in the diamond case."

"No doubt. Has a certain Pinkerton agent joined the investigation?"

"It would seem so."

"Will you be staying for supper?"

No good answer to that question. "I'm afraid not."

"Shall I leave the light on?"

Ouch. "Jealous, are we?"

"Don't you go along with your wild fantasies, Beau Longstreet. I know very well who you are. I simply need to remind myself when you presume to take liberties."

"Liberties. You mean like this?" He took her in his arms and kissed her over feeble protest.

"Oh!" She stomped her foot.

"Leave the light on," he whispered in her ear with a peck on the cheek.

Palace Hotel

She waited for him in the lobby, not feeling it proper to enter the salon alone. Lamp light flickered softly over elegant brocade furnishings and warm wood surroundings. A cheery fire crackled in a massive fireplace coming to the end of the long heating season. Longstreet entered the lobby, drawn to her in an instant like a moth to a flame. She smiled some mysterious recollection of a long ago fond memory. He returned her unspoken greeting, turning toward her on purposeful stride.

"Hello, handsome."

"You haven't changed."

"I should hope not. Buy a girl a drink?"

"Whiskey as I recall."

"You've a good memory. I seem to recall that one, too." She rose from her chair and took his arm.

The salon was dark and quiet early in the evening. Beau led her to a corner table and signaled the waiter. He held her chair.

"Two whiskies." The waiter scuttled off to the bar. "So, what brings you to Denver, and to what do I owe the pleasure of your company?"

She laughed. "Beau, this is Samantha. You know the answer to both those questions."

"You're here on your version of the jewel case, and since we are both surveilling the same suspects, you want to know what we know."

"You're so much more than a pretty face . . . so much more than that."

The waiter arrived with their drinks. Samantha lifted her glass.

"To old times."

Beau held her eyes. "To old times."

"Indeed." She took a swallow. "Now since we're on the subject, what do you know?"

"So, are we talking an exchange?"

"Of course."

"And you're working for his lordship."

"Reggie?" She shrugged.

"You first then. What have you got?"

She shook her head with a laugh. "Once burned, twice shy."

"That's it."

"All right. We know the gambit is *El Anillo*. The snitch they killed in the cemetery, the one they call the Weasel, was one of our informants."

"*El Anillo* is old news."

Samantha pursed her lips as though pained to continue. "The Weasel gave us Duval in the International Imports pinch."

"A pinch Reggie botched."

"Nobody's perfect. Your turn."

Beau swirled his whiskey in thought. "All right. For old times' sake. The geologist angle has something to do with a mine."

"A diamond mine?"

"Sounds like it."

"Where?"

He shrugged. "Now we're even."

"So, we watch and wait."

"Seems so."

She drained her glass. "Dinner?"

"Why not."

Dinner reminisced over the bearer-bond forgery case with some mutual reflections of which neither one spoke. Samantha waxed misty over her last bite of a raspberry tart.

"Your tie is crooked."

Beau remembered it coming undone. "I'll be taking it off soon."

"I know." She smiled.

"Not here. I've got to be going home."

"The widow. I think that's where we left things the last time. Any progress?"

"A little."

She shook her head. "A little. Beau, dear. Really?"

"The light is on."

"It is."

He closed the door and blew out the lamp. The stair creaked as he climbed.

Maddie glanced at her watch. Eight o'clock. She blew out the lamp, pulled the covers up to her chin, and smiled at the darkness.

Chapter Twenty-Four

Palace Hotel

The knock sounded like a pistol shot in the silence of the small room. Duval reached for his gun.

"Who is it?"

"Endicott."

He opened the door. The geologist stepped in, closing the door behind him.

"What's so urgent it couldn't wait until supper?"

"This." He handed over a telegram.

> *Meet Counselor U. P. Hotel Cheyenne.*
> *Prepared to validate claim.*
>
> *E.*

"Pack. We leave on the morning stage."

Great Western Detective League Office

Cane found Crook at his desk. Waning afternoon light colored the otherwise deserted office a tawny glow.

"One of our boys just bought two tickets on the morning stage to Cheyenne."

"What do you suppose that means?"

"It means we're going to Cheyenne. I'll let Longstreet know."

"You can't take the same stage."

"I know. If we leave now on horseback we should reach

Cheyenne within a few hours of when they do."

"What about our Pinkerton friends?"

"They may not know what's afoot. Trevane was still watching the hotel when I left."

"Good. Perchance we may get a step ahead of them. I'll notify the sheriff in Cheyenne and have him on the lookout for our suspects when they arrive. Check with his office when you arrive. He will see you get to where you need to be."

Palace Hotel

Samantha descended the circular stairway to the lobby dimly lit in morning light. Trevane sat in a corner near the fireplace under cover of reading a newspaper. She crossed the lobby to warm her hands by the fire.

"Any sign of our boys?"

The paper never moved. "No. It's odd, too. They usually have breakfast by now."

Samantha knit her brows. "I have a feeling the coffee may be getting cold."

"What?"

She crossed the lobby to the registration desk. The clerk brightened. She had that effect on men.

"I'd like to leave a message for a guest."

"Of course, madam."

He extended paper, pen, and ink. She scribbled and folded the note.

"Please see Mr. Duval gets this as soon as possible.

"Oh, I'm terribly sorry, madam. I'm afraid that won't be possible. Mr. Duval and Mr. Endicott checked out quite early this morning."

Damn.

Pinkerton Office

Trevane returned to the office at midday. He found Samantha

and Kingsley in the managing director's office.

"Two men matching the descriptions boarded the morning stage to Cheyenne. The next stage isn't until tomorrow morning."

Kingsley shook his head. "A day's head start; they could be anywhere by the time we catch up to them. Any sign of Crook's people?"

Trevane shook his head. "Our boys were the only two passengers. They must have given us all the slip."

"Don't be too sure," Samantha said. "Crook casts a wide net. If he knows where they've gone, I'm sure he will arrange a reception for them in Cheyenne. We'll try the sheriff when we get to Cheyenne. He may be able to put us back on the trail."

"Able and willing are two different things," Kingsley carped.

Samantha smiled. "Sometimes a little charm goes a long way."

Cane set a steady pace all the first night and through the next day, pausing only to rest the horses. A stage made the run from Denver to Cheyenne in two days with team changes every ten miles. With the advantage of a fourteen-hour head start, Cane hoped to cover the distance in no more than three. And so it was that, as the sun drifted beyond the western peaks at the end of the first day, Cane drew a halt in a rocky gulch, fully expecting the Cheyenne stage to overtake them. Within an hour the stage boiled by in a cloud of dust.

"There they go," Longstreet said.

"Crook's got them covered," Cane said.

Longstreet shook his head. "Clever the way this league of his works. For all the money and blather about 'The Eye that Never Sleeps,' Pinkerton can't match what he does."

"Money's the answer."

"How so?"

"Pinkerton keeps all the money in his pocket. Crook spreads it around. I didn't understand it at first, but I do now. That sheriff in Cheyenne is our friend. He won't give Pinkerton the time of day."

Longstreet nodded with a smile. He looked at the horses. "Smoke looks like he could go another couple of hours. My bay needs a blow. Let's take advantage of our friend and rest the horses a bit."

Cane stripped Smoke's lattigo. "You might make a trail man yet."

The stage run north to Cheyenne irked Samantha on more than one account. She hated the cold, rain, snow, heat, dust, and general discomfort of stage travel, along with the knowledge that all of it would have them arrive too late to their purpose. The only redeeming quality of this ride was the opportunity to observe Trevane. He was a handsome devil to say the least. And for all his "company policy" reservation, he had an eye for her. Company policy had its place. So did Longstreet. But a bird in the hand—Well this bird at least was worth . . . her thoughts drifted along to the jounce and sway of the coach.

Dust, dirt, the infernal rock and roll of the coach did nothing to deflect the attraction. Samantha Maples . . . well, women like her just didn't come along all that often. Trevane's thoughts meandered beyond her travel weeds. He pretended to doze of necessity to cover his interest.

She lifted her kerchief to her nose against the dust and smiled. Men in his condition . . . Her eyes filled with mirth—so simple really.

A half-day's ride from Cheyenne a second Denver stage barreled up the road behind them. Cane had an eye on their back trail that morning, fully expecting the next stage to come along and confirm his hunch. He signaled a halt and wheeled off the road.

"Here she comes," Cane said stepping down.

"Here who come?" Longstreet said.

"Our Pinkerton friends."

"Where?"

Cane lifted a chin down the road to the south. "Stage left Denver yesterday."

"What makes you think Pinkerton's on it?"

"Just a hunch. Keep a sharp eye."

Minutes later the Denver stage rolled by. Two passengers rode silhouetted in the dim confines of the coach muted in dust cloud.

"What do you think?" Cane said.

"Mount up. We're chasin' them now."

CHAPTER TWENTY-FIVE

U. P. Hotel
Cheyenne

Counselor arrived on the eastbound from San Francisco the day after Duval and Endicott registered at the U. P. Hotel. On their arrival at the stage office, they took no note of Sheriff Collin Firth and his deputy watching from across the street. The sheriff or one of his deputies, dressed in their Sunday best, occupied a corner of the hotel lobby ever since the pair arrived. Counselor took a suite and invited Duval and Endicott to join him in his small parlor.

"The San Francisco investors are prepared to go forward pending verification of the claim. New York will go along with the verification findings."

"Steps in the right direction, but we're not out of the woods yet," Endicott said.

"What do you mean?"

"The real test is who is to conduct the verification. What are his credentials? That will determine our ability to carry off the deception."

"What do you mean?"

"If they send us a geologist or gemologist, we'll be up against a man of serious expertise."

"How do you feel about a mining engineer?" Counselor said.

"Go on."

"Verification will be conducted by a Swede." Counselor

consulted his notes. "A mining engineer by the name of Jorgensen. He's no gemologist. His expertise will advise the investors the stones should be easily extracted."

Endicott smiled. "When might we expect him?"

"He should arrive on the eastbound train from San Francisco this afternoon. Make preparations for the three of you to leave for the claim in the morning."

Endicott and Duval returned to the hotel after arranging for horses at the livery and provisioning for the ride to the claim. Duval stopped in his tracks at the hotel door. He grabbed Endicott by the arm.

"What's the matter?" Endicott said.

"Him."

Endicott followed Duval's gaze to the tall man climbing the guest-room stairs carrying bags for himself and a beautiful woman. "What about him?"

"Pinkerton. He was in on the pinch for the International Importers job."

"Coincidence?"

"Not a chance. I need to lay low. So do you."

"What do we do about our mine engineer?"

"Have Counselor meet him."

Cane and Longstreet wheeled off the stage road to Sixteenth Street with the sun advanced overhead well past midday. Cane led the way west at a trot to the sheriff's office. They drew in at the rail and stepped down. They found the sheriff at his desk.

"Sheriff Firth, Briscoe Cane, Great Western Detective League. This is my partner, Beau Longstreet."

Firth extended a hand. "We've been expecting you boys."

"What have you to tell us of our suspects?"

"They arrived as expected. Registered at the U. P. Hotel.

We've had them under surveillance ever since. They spent the day today arranging livery for four horses and laying in supplies. Looks like they're planning to go somewhere."

"And meet someone." Cane nodded to himself. "Where are the horses liveried?"

"Cheyenne Corral. You passed it on your way into town."

"We'll stable our horses there and keep an eye on theirs. You maintain your watch at the hotel. Let us know if anything develops. Come on, Beau, we best stock up on supplies of our own. No tellin' how long we'll be on the trail."

"One more thing," Firth said.

Longstreet lifted an enquiring brow.

"Pinkerton paid me a visit earlier this afternoon."

"Not surprising. What did you tell them?"

"Nothing."

"Where are they now?"

"They were headed for the U. P. Hotel when they left here."

"So they likely know that Endicott and Duval are there."

"They're not registered under their real names."

"Maybe we're in luck."

Gray predawn light seeped into the livery stable loft. Cane lay awake listening. Longstreet snored softly nearby. Voices announced their approach. Cane nudged Longstreet awake. He touched a finger to his lips as the men entered the stable below.

"The four in the first stalls are ours. The piebald is the pack horse. Are you an accomplished horseman, Mr. Jorgensen?"

"Passable. And please, if ve are to be on the trail together some days, call me Sven."

"Very well then, Sven. The gray mare on the right is yours. Duval, you best take the big buckskin."

The soft slap of saddle blankets and groans of saddle leather took over for conversation as the men saddled their horses and loaded the pack horse.

Cane's mind raced to formulate a plan not to lose them in the time it took to saddle their horses. By the time creaking saddle leather told him they were mounting, he knew what to do. They'd no more than cleared the stable doors and turned west on Sixteenth when Cane scrambled down the loft ladder with Longstreet close behind.

"I'll follow on foot while you saddle the horses. Hurry."

Out the door, Cane kept to the street to avoid boot racket on the boardwalk. He followed along at a jog as the riders turned south at the depot. By the time he reached the depot, the riders were crossing the tracks headed into the hills south of town. Minutes later he could still make out dark specks in the shafts of dawning light when Longstreet jogged up the street leading Smoke.

CHAPTER TWENTY-SIX

Samantha rolled out of bed to stand at the window, fretting over how she might wheedle the information they sought out of a reluctant Cheyenne sheriff. The puzzle lacked inspiration until the need of it evaporated like morning dew. Two horsemen appeared along the depot platform. They crossed the tracks heading south into the hills. The scarecrow on the gray didn't catch her attention; the big fellow on the bay did. *Beau Longstreet. Where on earth? And why?*

She spun away from the window, into the hall and knocked on the door of the next room. The door swung open to a bleary-eyed, bare chested Trevor Trevane. The eyes cleared wide and round at the sight of her in her nightgown. He stepped back holding the door.

"Well, well, I was hoping you'd warm up to me. I hadn't expected it quite so soon."

She patted his chest with a slight shake of her head. "Let's not get ahead of ourselves, Trev. Look at this."

I am.

She led the way to the window. "There's the answer to our question."

"What question?"

"Where the suspects have gone. That's Beau Longstreet and Briscoe Cane riding into the hills."

"Him again."

"Get yourself dressed. Get down to the livery and rent us a

137

couple of horses. Meet me at the general store. I'll provision us. We should be on their trail in two or three hours."

"We? You fixin' to go? That's rough country out there."

"Don't be an ass. Now get moving." She started for the door.

"One last question?"

She paused.

"How far ahead is ahead of ourselves?"

"I'll keep you posted," trailed over her shoulder.

"Of that you can be sure."

The door clicked closed behind her. She smiled.

Jeweled Garden

Endicott drew rein at the foot of a gentle slope on the bank of a creek.

"We base camp here."

"Where is the claim?" Jorgensen said.

"The west boundary runs along the west creek bank there." Endicott pointed the engineer along the far bank. "The east boundary runs up the slope taking in those black rock formations. Geological conditions there are what first caught my attention to the possibility of gemological formation."

"I see. Interesting."

They swung down.

"Put up the horses and start us a fire, Duval. I'll show Sven here around."

This manservant arrangement has gone about as far as a man can stand. "Yes, suh."

Endicott led Jorgensen along the creek bank, pausing at a well-chosen spot.

"Keep a sharp eye here. Erosion from the spring runoff can dislodge stones. It's possible to find them lying in the creek bed." He swept an arm over the hillside. "Further up, we follow the rock formations. That usually takes a bit of digging."

"Vhat is this?"

The mine engineer knelt on the creek bank and picked a glittering stone out of the shallows. He held it up to fading afternoon light. "Vhat a vonderful find." He offered Endicott the stone.

"Keep it. It's yours. There's plenty more where that came from as you'll see in the next few days."

The Swede pocketed the diamond appreciatively, estimating he'd more than doubled his fee for the project.

Longstreet and Cane had made no attempt to cover their tracks. Trevane had no difficulty following them. He hoped his field craft impressed Samantha. In addition to all her other qualities, she proved a competent horsewoman and a pleasant addition to an expedition like this. As the sun drifted west, they struck a stream bordered by a grove of aspen. Sign including a scorched-stone fire basin suggested someone may have camped there the previous evening. Trevane stepped down.

"We'll camp here." He offered Samantha a hand down.

She pretended not to notice. "I'll stir up a fire while you tend the horses."

"Don't light it until it gets dark. We're close enough to Longstreet and Cane, I don't want to risk putting up smoke sign before sunset."

Later, fatback, biscuits, and stewed tomatoes made for a nourishing supper after a long day on the trail. The sky broke out in a blanket of stars while crickets and frogs chattered back and forth across the gurgle of the creek. Evening breeze freshened the heat of the day.

Samantha yawned. "Been a long day. Think I'll turn in." She spread her blanket. Trevane did the same. She watched as he untied a lariat from his saddle and circled his sleeping ground with it. He lay down and tugged the blanket over him.

"What's the rope for?"

"Snakes."

"Snakes?"

"They won't cross it."

She glanced at her saddle. No lariat. "Where's my rope?"

"You mean you didn't bring one?"

"You saddled the horses."

"Must have forgot. I 'spect I could make a little room here."
He lifted his blanket.

She glanced from his invitation to her blanket. *What's a girl
to do?* She wriggled in beside him.

"Are we catching up yet?" Trevane asked.

"I'm keeping you posted."

"You are."

"I know. Are you sure this rope thing works?"

Jeweled Garden

Morning sun rode on into midday. Cane drew rein, cresting a
ridge. He wheeled Smoke back off the skyline and stepped
down. He bellied up to the crest of the ridge. Longstreet crawled
up beside him.

"What is it?"

"There." Cane lifted his chin to the south. "See that aspen
thicket? They's four horses picketed in them trees."

"Any sign of our boys?"

Cane shook his head. "Not from here. What do you suppose
they're doing camped out in the middle of nowhere?"

"Lookin' for a diamond mine," Longstreet said.

"You really think that's the play? Gold, sure; silver, maybe;
diamonds . . . I just don't know. Never heard of such a thing."

"We heard the Cajun and the tall one talking about a mine.
We don't know who the third jasper is or what they're up to. We
need to get a closer look."

"Cain't just ride on in there," Cane mused under a furrowed

brow. "Too much open country; we're bound to be seen. Wait—that's it."

"What's it?"

"Come on." Cane scrambled back to Smoke and swung into the saddle.

Longstreet followed. "Come on where?"

"Let's go get seen."

"Seen? That don't make sense."

"There's a difference between passers-by and pursuers. Pursuers is threatening. Passers-by is seen passing by."

Cane led the way east below the crest of the ridge. He turned south well wide of the object of their pursuit, continuing in a southeasterly direction until the thicket and hillside disappeared from view. Then he eased their way southwest toward a wash and a ridgeline east of the suspected diamond prospectors' campsite.

Giving the campsite a wide berth they climbed into the hills above. They rode into a stream-fed thicket in an arroyo. Cane stepped down.

"We leave the horses here and move in on foot."

They unsaddled the horses and picketed them in the trees. Cane drew his Henry from the saddle boot and led the climb up-slope to the west.

Cane eased their way down the mountain side toward the suspects' campsite, reckoning they had to be somewhere up-slope above them. He did his best to keep their presence under cover of rocks, trees, and ravines as he picked his way slowly downhill. They might have stumbled over their quarry if it hadn't been for the crack of steel on rock. They came upon Endicott and the unknown third man hacking shale around the base of a large, black rock formation.

"Vhat is this? Another vone." The Swede scraped a stone out

of the rock. "Another! And another! This is the richest strike I have ever experienced of any kind." He poured a fist full of stones into a small leather pouch and hung a small pick on his belt.

"Can you develop it?" Endicott said.

"Develop it? It vill practically develop itself."

"What more do we need to do here?"

"I've seen enough. Ve must return to Cheyenne in the morning. I vill send my report to the investors. Ve must begin this remarkable project at vonce."

Endicott led the way down the hill toward their camp.

Cane and Longstreet watched them go.

"What do you make of that?" Cane said.

"Sounds like the stranger is verifying the gem strike for prospective investors."

"Could make some folks a lot of money if the strike is as rich as the stranger believes it is."

Longstreet squinted at the two figures retreating down the slope toward their camp. "Could also make *El Anillo* a lot of money if investors bought into a mine salted with fenced stones from a run of jewel robberies."

"Call me a poor, dumb country bounty hunter, but Longstreet, you just might be onto something there. Makes more sense than the first precious gem strike ever reported in these parts."

"We move in tonight?" Longstreet said.

"I don't think so. There's more to this than meets the eye. It doesn't smell right. People doin' the dirty work out here in the middle of nowhere aren't the brains behind *El Anillo*. We'll let the Colonel make the call, but this time I think we play for the big fish. Now let's get back to the horses before night falls on this mountain."

Chapter Twenty-Seven

Jeweled Garden

Next morning Cane and Longstreet picked up their back trail down to the foothills. They swung west toward the claim site, pausing to wait for the prospectors to depart.

"Now let's have a look at what they're up to," Cane said, nudging Smoke across the face of the slope.

Trevane did his best to keep his attention on the trail while his mind wandered back over the unexpected turn taken the night before. He'd tossed an amorous loop and lassoed a most pleasant surprise. The sound of horses up the trail brought him back to the present. He drew rein.

"Someone's coming." He glanced around. A dense thicket grew out of a rock fall east of the trail. "This way."

They cleared cover and dismounted. Moments later Endicott and the mine engineer came down the narrow trail in single file followed by Duval, leading the pack horse. Trevane reached for his gun.

"What do you think you're doing with that?" Samantha hissed.

"Take 'em."

"On what charge, suspicion?"

They let the riders pass out of hearing.

"Why do you suppose Longstreet and Cane didn't take them?"

Trevane shrugged.

"There's more at play here than a couple of jewelry store robberies."

"So what do we do now? Follow their back trail to see what they've been up to, or follow them back to Cheyenne?"

"I don't think we'll find much up that back trail except Longstreet and Cane. There are other ways to find out what they're up to." She smiled a knowing smile, stepped into her saddle, and wheeled her horse up the trail to Cheyenne.

Cane and Longstreet picketed their horses in the aspen thicket grown up beside the creek. Cane set off along the creek bank, Longstreet up the slope. They'd seen two of them digging around the base of a large, black rock formation. Now Longstreet noticed the hillside was filled with them. He inspected the base of one close at hand. Loose shale struck him as odd. Hard-packed made more sense. He knelt and scraped at the loose stones. Something sparkled ruby red in the light. The stone was the size of his thumb nail. He picked it up. What had the unknown stranger said? *The richest strike he'd ever experienced.* A strike in precious gems? What did that have to do with jewel robbery? Nothing, unless you were trying to create the appearance of a *rich strike.* His gut told him his earlier speculation was right. If stones like these were throwaway bait, somebody was about to lose a lot of money.

She rose up on her hind legs from behind the boulder, near seven feet in height, her massive head full of drooling fangs, her pie-plate paws full of claws. Longstreet felt his knees go weak. The pocket pistol in his shoulder holster wouldn't give her a pause. She bounded to the top of the boulder with a roar, ready to pounce. She leaped.

Longstreet spun away to his left and scrambled up the side of the boulder, gaining the height she'd given away. The advantage proved short lived. He'd put himself between the angry sow and two cubs. *Shit!*

She righted herself and charged up the slope toward him.

Longstreet leaped down from the boulder and took off at a run. He ran toward the creek, too far away. No chance he could outrun a determined pursuit. The vicious growls she threw after him sounded plenty determined.

A bumblebee buzzed overhead followed by the throaty crack of a Henry long rifle. The heavy slug exploded rock chips in her path.

Longstreet didn't dare look back. He continued running as fast as his watery knees would carry him.

The Henry barked again. He risked a glance back. She stood on her hind legs clawing the air, then settled down with a dismissive snort, satisfied she'd run off the threat. She ambled back to her cubs.

Longstreet skidded to a stop, chest heaving, eyes round as saucers. Cane's shoulders shook in suppressed laughter, his eyes moist with mirth.

"What's so funny?" Longstreet managed a gasp.

"The look on your face."

"There's no way you could have seen at that distance."

"I mean now. Might you be needin' a clean pair of long-handles?"

CHAPTER TWENTY-EIGHT

Shady Grove

"I received a wire as to the circumstances surrounding the investigation forthwith to their return to Cheyenne. I concurred with Cane's course in angling for the big fish."

He seemed in good spirits today, more energetic in his recounting of the case. I glanced at my watch and then at my notes. "This might be a good place to stop for today."

He lifted a suspicious brow. "Some important engagement to attend to have we?"

I glanced over his shoulder, conspiratorially. The solarium was deserted save for the two of us. "I need to get to Brumble Jewelers before they close."

"Near to a purchase then."

I nodded.

"A stone or a band?"

"A small stone."

"An investment. To what do we owe this flush of prosperity?"

"Hardly a flush—I've only just received a royalty draft from my publisher."

"You prosper to investment-grade jewels whilst I linger here wasting in these dreary confines."

"Oh, come now, Colonel. You're comfortable and suitably medicated." I glanced at the bulge under his lap robe for emphasis.

"I'll be the judge of suitability. Now when should I expect my caregiver to lapse into a swoon of useless delirium?"

"Soon."

"How soon?"

"Soon is the best I can do for now. Not so soon if I don't get to the store before it closes."

"Off with you then. I can't abide the notion of standing in the way of nuptial bliss."

Brumble Jewelers

I tucked the small package in my coat pocket and left the store for the walk home. Once I'd decided to forego the traditional gold band in favor of the bold statement of a diamond, the second departure from tradition came easier. The filigreed silver setting set off the diamond beautifully. Selecting silver over gold helped keep the extravagance bordering on affordable. For better or worse the decisions were made. Now the question, when? *Soon. How soon is soon? Where? In what circumstances? The questions kept coming. Is there nothing about so blissful a decision to come easily?*

U. P. Hotel
Cheyenne

Late-afternoon sun washed Kingsley's parlor suite in fading golden light. His lordship held court, listening to Samantha and Trevane recount their pursuit of the suspects. He stroked his moustache as Trevane brought the report to its conclusion.

"The two principals have kept pretty much to themselves since we returned. The third man had breakfast with a fourth unknown yesterday morning. They discussed what appeared to be a report of some sort. The new man took it when they finished, and both took the westbound yesterday, though it didn't appear they traveled together."

"And we don't know who these last two are or how they fit into our case."

"We don't know much," Trevane said. "The third man registered under the name Sven Jorgensen. The fourth registered as a Mr. Kendrick."

"Not much to go on."

"I'm afraid not."

"It would seem our worthy competitors may have somewhat better information than we at the moment. Do we know where they are?"

"Checked into the hotel but laying very low," Samantha said.

"Might you use your influence with Longstreet to gain some insight?"

"I can try. He's gotten cagy when he knows he's being played."

"See what you can do. Perhaps you will have something to report tomorrow. That will be all for now."

Outside in the hall, Trevane caught Samantha in a sidelong glance. "What sort of influence do you have over Longstreet?"

She patted his cheek. "If you'll excuse me, I have a note to pen."

She set off down the hall. Trevane followed the saucy turn of her hip. He felt her influence and a certain reluctance to see her ply it on Longstreet, whatever that meant.

Samantha arrived in the salon uncharacteristically early. Her gaze swept the dimly lit elegance to see if Longstreet might already be there.

"Looking for someone?"

She turned to find the voice belonged to the one calling himself Endicott. She contained her good fortune with an inviting smile. "Only a colleague."

"Thoughtless to keep a beautiful woman waiting. Might I buy you a drink until his manners improve?"

"Did I say it was a gentleman?"

"I merely assumed."

"A man would, but I'll allow you to buy me that drink by way of amends."

"Amends. We've yet to be introduced and already I've muddled it."

"Samantha Maples." She extended a hand.

"Jeremiah Endicott." He held her hand, making a point.

He led her to a corner table and signaled the bartender.

"What'll it be?"

"Sherry," Samantha said.

"Whiskey for me."

"What brings a lovely thing like you to Cheyenne?"

"Textiles."

"You're a drummer?"

"Drummer's assistant."

"What does a drummer's assistant do?"

"I supply good taste."

"Good taste."

"Of course. Shopkeepers know nothing of women's taste in fabrics. I simply advise them on the wisest choices for their inventories."

"And these shopkeepers don't see through this arrangement?"

"The shopkeepers don't know."

Endicott chuckled. "Clever."

Longstreet appeared in the batwings as the bartender arrived with their drinks. She caught his eye. He read hers and made off to a far corner table.

"And you. What brings you to Cheyenne?"

"I'm a geologist, currently engaged in a mining exploration."

"Gold?"

He leaned forward. "Better. Diamonds."

Her hand covered her mouth in wide-eyed, feigned surprise. "I should think those samples are far superior to textiles."

He chuckled. "Indeed. Perhaps I can come up with one for you, should your colleague not detain you so long you're unable to join me for supper."

"My colleague will understand. Hold your thought while I see to it."

She crossed the salon to Longstreet's table.

"Something more interesting has come up I see," Longstreet said.

"Why Beau Longstreet, could that be jealousy?"

He smiled.

"As a matter of fact, it's a chance meeting too good to pass up."

"We'll have much to discuss later then."

"I knew you'd understand." She patted his cheek.

CHAPTER TWENTY-NINE

Late-morning sun warmed Kingsley's suite. Samantha laid a glittering diamond on the table. "Investment capital. He's awaiting the capital to launch a mining operation."

"Investment capital?"

"That's what he said."

Trevane stood at the window, frosty in spite of summer heat. Samantha found his pique amusing.

"Talkative fellow for someone in that sort of business," Trevane said.

"Anything to impress a lady."

"And did he?"

She smiled a smile that said "I'd-pat-your-cheek-if-Reggie-weren't-here" and let him go at that.

"Rather a good day's work, Samantha. I should think we've one-up'd the competition on this one," Kingsley said.

"One can't be sure until I've sounded out Longstreet. We were forced to forego our meeting by chance opportunity. I intend to meet him later today."

"I worry all this chance opportunity might wear you out," Trevane said.

"All in a day's work." She scooped up the diamond.

"Where are you going with that?" Kingsley said.

"I need something to give up to Beau."

"Beau. All in a day's work," Trevane muttered.

★ ★ ★ ★ ★

Longstreet sat at a back corner table in the salon, waiting for Samantha to make her expected entrance. She swept through the batwings and crossed the dimly lit room without the slightest hesitation straight for his table. He stood to hold her chair.

"Am I that predictable?"

She smiled. "Woman's intuition."

He signaled the bartender. Two whiskies and a bottle appeared.

"Man after my own heart."

"Woman after mine."

"You noticed."

"So did he?" He lifted his chin over her shoulder.

Trevane sat at the bar, watching with no pretense of disinterest.

"It seems you've taken on a minder," Beau said.

"I don't recall doing so. Sweet attention, though."

"Speaking of sweet attentions, what did you find out from our friend last night?"

"Too much history between us to play parlor games."

"We do have a history, don't we?"

"Don't distract me. Are we talking an exchange?"

"It depends on what Sir Reggie has given you leave to give."

She placed a small diamond on the table.

"Old news."

"He's a geologist, working on a mining project."

"That squares with what Cain and I saw. He and the Cajun were showing the third man around what must be their claim."

"They're waiting for some investors to come in to finance the mining operation. So far, we've got nothing beyond suspicion in the jewelry store holdups."

"So where does that leave us?"

"I don't know about you, but we wait and watch." She

drained her glass.

Longstreet refilled both glasses.

"So, are you going to buy a girl supper whilst we while away our waiting and watching?"

"Do you suppose your minder will approve?"

She shrugged. "What about yours?"

"Mine?"

"Don't be coy with me. This is Samantha, remember? The widow of course."

"Maddie's not my minder. I'm beneath her."

"At least you're making progress."

"Beneath her dignity."

"Then I don't know which of you is the greater fool. She for not knowing what she's missing, or you for knowing and not taking advantage of the opportunities before you."

"Seems like that's where we left it last time."

"It does, doesn't it. Thanks for the drink."

She left the table for a grinning Trevane.

Hacienda Carnicero
Santa Fe

Sunset. Don Victor feasted his eyes on waning light, turning the mountain caps pink and orange high above a carpet of purple and blue shadow. He savored the easy draw and mellow drift of an aromatic cigar at the end of the day. He seldom let business interfere with these moments. Today he made an exception. The import of Escobar's report satisfied a hunger more needful than the beauty of the mountains.

The Counselor formed two companies. Jeweled Garden Partners and Consolidated Mining. Shares in Jeweled Garden Partners would be sold to the investors. Jeweled Garden Partners would then contract with Consolidated Mining to develop the claim in return for five percent of the gross receipts. Contract terms would leave the appearance of a river of profits to the investors. Of course, the river would go dry the moment Jeweled Garden Partners' drafts credited to Consolidated Mining's account. Counselor met with the San Francisco investors, armed with the engineer Jorgensen's report. Escobar continued.

"The engineer reported the claim the richest he had ever seen. He found conditions to develop the field most favorable. The San Francisco Investors agreed to fund the partners group. Their intentions were declared to the New York investors. Counselor is awaiting receipt of their funds. He suggests we meet in Cheyenne to disburse the proceeds."

The Don smiled. *"Bueno."*

"Will you travel to Cheyenne?"

He shook his head. "No; you will go to collect our share."

"How are the shares to be distributed?"

"One hundred thousand each to Endicott, the safe *hombre*, and Counselor. Bring the remaining five hundred thousand to me."

"The Don is most generous."

"Generous to a fault. I am but an honorable thief." He laughed.

CHAPTER THIRTY

U. P. Hotel
Cheyenne
Cane dozed in his room. He snapped awake at a sharp knock at the door. He rolled off the bed instinctively reaching for his Forehand & Wadsworth Bull Dog on the nightstand.

"Who is it?"

"Longstreet. Open up."

Cane admitted his partner, tucking the Bull Dog in his backup rig.

"Something's up."

"Like what?"

"The *El Anillo* enforcer just showed up in the hotel lobby. He sent a message to a guest named Kendrick."

"How do you know?"

"I overheard the desk clerk send the bell man up with the note."

"Did he recognize you?"

"Didn't see me. I watched from the salon. They no more than sent the message up to this Kendrick's room when word came back to send him up. They're in a suite on the third floor."

"Any sign of our other two friends?"

"Which two?"

"Endicott and Duval."

"Not so far."

"While we're at it, any sign of Samantha or Trevane?"

155

"They've been watching the lobby just like we have, but I didn't see any sign of either of them down there just now."

"Seems odd."

"It does, unless . . ."

"Unless what?" Cane said.

"Unless they're in a position to know something we don't."

"You think she . . ."

"Could be. You take the trail south. I'll keep an eye on things here."

Cane pulled up his suspenders and strapped on his rig.

Polished wood furnishings in the parlor suite gleamed late-afternoon light creamed through lace curtain. Counselor yawned, weary from the effects of travel. Very soon the deal would be done. He'd gone to San Francisco with the mining engineer's report. The investors were only too pleased to purchase shares. Word was sent to New York. The report was all Gould needed to hear. The New York money came in by wire within days. He'd come back to Cheyenne with the necessary drafts to close the deal and disappear into retirement. A knock at the door brought his wait to an end. He smiled as he crossed the suite. At least he'd chosen the venue for this meeting away from the ferret's vile brothel.

Endicott and Duval arrived first, followed minutes later by Escobar.

"Everything concluded as expected?" Escobar said.

Counselor nodded as he opened his case. He drew out four cashier's drafts. He handed the first for five hundred thousand to Escobar. He passed one hundred thousand each to Endicott and Duval. He held up the fourth for all to see.

"My share. I believe that puts everything in order."

Heads nodded all around the table.

"Now, I suggest we leave one by one, using both the front

and rear entrances."

Escobar rose and departed.

Cane waited at the east end of town hidden in an alley where he could observe the stage road south. As expected the *El Anillo* man wheeled south of Sixteenth Street at a lope down the stage road to Denver. Cane let him go some distance before stepping into Smoke's saddle. This trail had a distance to go before the need of close pursuit.

Endicott and Duval departed Counselor's suite.

"Well, I guess this is it," Endicott said, pausing at the door to his room. "I'm leaving on the train tomorrow."

Duval extended his hand with a smile. "Being at your service might have been a pain in the ass, but at least it pays well."

Endicott took his hand. "If you hurry, you can still catch the afternoon stage."

The big black man disappeared down stairs to the lobby.

Endicott unlocked the door to his room and stepped in.

"That was quick," she said.

Longstreet lounged in a far corner of the lobby, hidden in the pages of a Cheyenne daily. Duval bounced down the stairs and headed for the door. Longstreet tossed his newspaper aside and followed to the door. Duval stepped onto the boardwalk, blinded for an instant by bright sunlight.

"Stop right where you are."

He cut his eyes to the Pinkerton man. "What are you doing here?"

"Waiting for you. You're under arrest," Trevane said.

"On what charge?"

"We'll start with the Cheyenne jeweler holdup. You can fill in the blanks from there."

"You shouldn't spend so much time in the sun. It addles the brain."

"I don't think so."

"You haven't a shred of proof."

"Oh no? How do you explain that diamond bauble you dropped on the little tart at the Velvet Ribbon?"

Duval scowled.

"Hands behind your back." Trevane cuffed his wrists and patted him down. He recovered a nickel plated .32 with ivory handles and a cashier's draft for one hundred thousand dollars. "Walking around money?"

"Where's Kingsley?"

"He'll be along. What do you want with him?"

"Maybe we can make a deal."

"Maybe we can. Let's get you locked up first."

Longstreet turned to the registration counter.

Chapter Thirty-One

Samantha stretched out, porcelain on a red-velvet settee. "I should have thought it would take longer to finance development of a mine."

Endicott loosened his tie. "That's why you do fabrics and I do gems."

"Oh this?" She playfully plucked at a bit of lace. "Chemise."

"I see."

"I'm sure you do."

He slipped off his coat and tossed it over a chair.

She lifted her chin to his shoulder rig. "I was expecting assault with a friendly weapon. That looks a bit deadly."

The rig followed the coat to the chair. He turned toward her only to find himself staring down the muzzle of her gun.

"Pinkerton. You're under arrest."

He laughed. "On what charge?"

"Dealing in stolen merchandise and fraud should do for a start."

"I don't know what you're talking about."

"I'm talking about salting a worthless mining claim with stolen gemstones for the purpose of defrauding unsuspecting investors. I suspect we'll find their draft in your coat pocket, your share of the take."

A knock at the door caught both by surprise. Endicott sprang like a cat, knocking Samantha's pistol from her hand. He grabbed her around the waist and dragged her back to the chair, where he retrieved his gun.

"Who is it?"

"Room service."

"I didn't order room service."

"Mr. Duval sends his compliments."

"You'll arouse suspicion if you don't accept." She planted a seed.

"All right then, since you're so adept at putting men off in your unmentionables, you accept it. Just remember this gun is pointed at the back of your head. Make one false move and . . ."

She opened the door to Longstreet and an iced bucket of champagne. His eyes smiled. She let her eyes interrupt with unspoken alarm.

"Please give Mr. Duval our grateful regards." She accepted the bucket with a slight tilt of her head behind her and closed the door. "Care for a glass?"

"Get dressed. We're leaving."

Longstreet strolled purposefully down the corridor to the fire door at the back of the building. He stepped out on the landing and looked up, measuring the height and overhang of the roof.

She collected her things and started to dress, buying time.

"You think you're just going to walk out of here?"

"I better, for your sake."

She slipped into her dress and bent to lace up her shoes. The window exploded into the room. Endicott wheeled on the intruder. Samantha's arm flashed up, deflecting his shot into the ceiling. Longstreet lunged into him with the force of a battering ram, knocking him backward. His arm cracked against the door frame, scattering the gun from his hand. They crashed to the floor in a heap. Longstreet jumped to his feet. Samantha trained her gun on the stunned swindler.

"You make quite an entrance," she said.

"That's all the thanks I get?"

"Heavens no. You shall have all the thanks you please."

Endicott shook his head, looking from one to the other.

Sheriff's Office
Cheyenne

Trevane and Samantha stood at the cell door. Duval sulked on his bunk in the dull gray of early evening.

"Tell us about the people behind this scheme," Trevor said.

"I've got nothing to say."

"You know it will go easier on you if you cooperate."

"Where's Kingsley?"

"He'll be along."

"Maybe we can make a deal."

"I'm afraid you're well past the scot-free deal you've got in mind," Trevane said.

"You want to make a deal, bargain for a lighter sentence, or time off for good behavior?" Samantha said.

"I got nothing to say."

"Why protect these people?"

He glanced up, brows bunched. "The Ring's got long arms."

"C'mon, Trevor. We're wasting our time. Let's see if lover boy over there is in a more talkative mood."

Endicott paced in his cell at the far end of the cell block.

"Comfy?" Samantha said.

"Hardly. I demand to see a lawyer. You've got nothing on me."

"As of now we've got two hundred thousand dollars of probable cause. As for the lawyer, all in good time. Now, if you were to cooperate, the court might go easy on you," Trevane said.

"Cooperate how?"

"Who's backing this scheme?" Samantha asked.

"I don't know."

"Come on, Jeremiah. This is Samantha. I do textiles, remember?"

"I remember I should be more careful of the ladies I bed."

"What and miss all this fun?"

Trevane scowled.

"Now be a good boy and tell us who's behind this scheme?"

"What's in it for me if I do?"

"A recommendation for leniency."

"What's that worth?"

She shrugged. "Five, ten years, maybe a suspended sentence if the information is good enough."

Silence.

Samantha caught Trevane's eye. "We're wasting our time, Trev. C'mon." She turned to go.

"All right," Endicott said. "Counselor brought in San Francisco and New York investors."

Trevane pulled out a pad and pencil.

"How many investors?"

"I don't really know. We met two of them."

"Who?"

"Collis Crocker and Mark Leland. They're San Francisco money. I don't know the New York money."

"Just how much money are we talking?" Samantha said.

"Eight hundred thousand."

Her jaw dropped. "You and Duval each got one hundred. What happened to the rest?"

"Counselor got one hundred. The Don got the rest."

"Counselor?"

"Called himself Kendrick when it suited him. He filed the claim, drew up the papers, acted like the Don's lawyer."

"And this Don?"

"Don Victor Carnicero. Counselor worked for him. So did Escobar."

"The ferret?" Trevane said.

"That's him."

"And Don Victor heads *El Anillo*?"

He nodded.

"Where do we find Don Victor?"

He shrugged. "My orders came from Santa Fe."

CHAPTER THIRTY-TWO

Shady Grove

"Cane arrived in Denver on the trail of the *El Anillo* man. He'd ridden south at a comfortable pace with no apparent fear of being followed. He spent a night in Denver at a second-class bordello. Cane took the opportunity to have me wire Longstreet with instructions to meet him in Santa Fe."

Another fit of coughing cut off his train of thought.

"I believe I have enough for this day, Colonel."

He glanced at the slant of the sun. "Don't coddle me for a little rasp in my throat, boy."

"I wouldn't dream of it."

"No, I suppose not. Too busy dreaming about a certain young lady. Any progress on your purchase?"

I patted my coat pocket by way of reply. He lifted a brow.

"Might we soon have an announcement?"

I touched a forefinger to my lips and smiled.

"I see. Wellst fore-warned is fore-armed. I'm quite sure she will be in a euphoric bubble at the news."

Truth be told, I was a bit nervous over the big question. I'd labored long in my thinking over the how and the where of the asking. Then of course there was the matter of what she might say. I couldn't quite muster up the Colonel's certainty of her acceptance.

"Robert."

Brought me back to the present.

164

"I'll be rolling along to my cell now. Do me a kindness and put yourself out of this misery soon. Lord knows I may not have enough time left to witness your engagement if you don't get off your reticent arse and get on with it!"

"I thought you were concerned it might affect the efficiency of your care."

"I can live with the inevitability of decline. It's the suspense that is killing me."

Properly chastened, I left.

I waited nervously for Penny to finish for the day. I occupied my time rehearsing my lines. One would think a writer should have no difficulty mustering four simple words. "Will," "you," and "me" came easily enough; it was that terribly important third word that terrified me. I thought I might choke on it. Then there was the where of the asking. I sorted through and discarded dozens of possibilities to no good eventuality. In the end, in a near state of panic, I settled on the ice cream parlor where we had our first sundae together. Caramel and chocolate seemed to suit the occasion in a poetic sort of nostalgia. At least I hoped so. And then the moment of truth arrived. She looked lovely leaving the Shady Grove Rest Home and Convalescent Center, even dressed in her institutional uniform. She took my arm with one of her Mona Lisa smiles, and somehow I knew things would work out.

She didn't ask where we were going as we walked down the hill into town. She didn't seem surprised when I suggested a sundae, or even raise a question when I guided her to the back corner booth we'd taken that first time. It wasn't until we'd ordered our usual—her caramel, my chocolate—that she seemed to notice.

"Robert, do you remember the first time we came here?"

I nodded. She chuckled.

"The Colonel practically asked me for you."

"I was a mite shy."

"A mite? Good heavens."

My anxiety built as I contemplated my next move. A reprieve arrived in the form of our ice cream.

"We owe him a good deal," Penny said.

"We do." Wistful my Mona Lisa.

"Our introduction. Your writing. He's had a hand in all of it."

She was worried about him, as was I. But this line of conversation did not lead to the joyful conclusion I'd planned. It was now or never.

"Perhaps we should owe him something more."

She lifted a brow in her quizzical way. I felt my throat tighten.

"Penny O'Malley, will you m-marry me?"

Her eyes shot round as I produced the ring from my pocket. It turns out I wasn't the only one with vocal problems. Her eyes went misty.

"Oh, Robert . . . Yes, oh yes! . . . It's beautiful!"

I don't recall much of the walk to her rooming house. We tarried on the porch until we might wear out our lips with kissing. For all my impossible stewing and fretting it seemed I'd managed to turn it out right in the end.

Shady Grove

I found the Colonel taking mountain air on a warm, sunny morning the following Saturday. I'd been in high spirits the whole week and expected the rest of the world to be as pleased with itself as I was. I wasn't prepared for his greeting.

"Now you've gone and done it, boy. I hope you're pleased with yourself."

"Gone and done what?"

"Rendered that poor girl a near useless puddle of emotion."

"Oh that. As a matter of fact, I am rather pleased with myself over that."

"You might at least have given me fair warning so I could have steeled myself in preparation."

"You're the one who told me to get on with it as I recall. And for all that, what possible preparation might you have required?"

"For the complete loss of discipline in my schedule."

"I didn't think you liked the discipline in your schedule."

"I don't appreciate being deprived of my displeasure. It assures me I maintain some level of delusion as to dignity."

"Seems as though you've maintained sufficient displeasure to carry on."

"Bah! She floats about, dreamy-eyed, gazing at that bauble you invested in. At the moment I'm quite sure it's worth well more than she is."

"Hardly. Penny's worth is far beyond my humble expressions of love."

"Good heavens, you're as addled as she. Did you even bother to bring your note pad and pencil today?"

"Of course I did." I proudly produced my pad from its coat pocket and patted for the pencil. I patted some more.

"I'm sure the warden out front will loan you a stub."

I grimaced. Red faced and chagrined I slunk to the reception desk to beg a writing instrument. The attendant in reception greeted me with one of those conspiratorial smiles women seem able to manufacture when invested with some juicy tidbit of gossip or scandalous news they feel privileged to possess.

"Lovely ring, Robert. All the girls are positively green with envy. Might you have any unattached brothers?"

I shook my head, thanked her for the pencil, and returned to a self-satisfied expression of "see-I-told-you-so."

"Now then, where were we?"

Grateful for his attention to the business at hand I consulted my notes.

"Endicott confessed the scheme and gave up the Don as the

mastermind."

"Ah, yes. We, of course, did not know that at first. We learned as much when, as a matter of course, I reported developments in Cheyenne to Malthus in San Francisco. He requested our introduction to the sheriff in Cheyenne by return wire and decamped forthwith to interview the prisoners."

CHAPTER THIRTY-THREE

Sheriff's Office
Cheyenne
Click. Endicott snapped out of a shallow sleep. The cell block enveloped him in pitch black, save the barest glow of starlight drifting through barred upper windows. He listened. Had he heard it, or might it have been a dream? Iron creaked. *That's no dream.* Couldn't be a jailer; he'd have a lamp or a lantern.

"Duval, is that you?" he hissed.

Shuffling.

"Quiet," bright eyes said in the dark stillness.

Endicott rolled off his bunk with groan of spring. "How'd you get out?"

"Hairpin," white teeth said. "I'm a box man, remember?"

"Get me out then."

"Sorry."

"Sorry? You mean you're going to leave me here?"

"Nothing personal. I just don't figure to be anywhere close when *El Anillo* comes for you."

"What do you mean?"

"I mean, it don't pay to sing on those boys. They have their ways. The law dogs can promise you the moon with a fence around it for protection; it don't matter. You a dead man, Jeremiah. Nice knowin' you."

He shuffled off, no more than faint whisper on stone.

"Duval, wait! Don't leave me."

The office door clicked. Hinges complained. He was gone.

Starlight lit the office. Duval rummaged through a cabinet to find his gun rig and wallet. He checked the street. Quiet. He slipped out of the office and into the nearest alley. He made his way to the livery stable, selected a sturdy gelding, and saddled him. He rode south out of town, losing his tracks in the stage road to Denver. He reckoned the Don for his best chance of escape.

Pinkerton Office
Denver

Kingsley fingered his moustache as Trevane poured over his notes reporting on the Endicott interrogation. Samantha listened absently, bored from having heard it all before.

"He was able to give us no more on the Don than the fact his orders came from Santa Fe."

"What did you get from our Cajun friend?"

"Nothing. He clammed up tight."

"Interesting, though not surprising."

"Why not?" Samantha said.

"You recall the Weasel informant you gave up to Longstreet. He offered information on the mysterious *El Anillo*. He suffered a rather untimely demise, featuring a slit throat, 'silence' carved in his chest, and the loss of his ring finger."

"So, other than suddenly nauseated, where does that leave us?"

"We have a partial recovery, two hundred thousand of an eight-hundred-thousand-dollar loss. I shall have the San Francisco office notify the San Francisco investors—Crocker and Leland I believe you said were their names. Perhaps they can identify the New York investors."

Trevane nodded.

"Further to that, we have a shadowy trail that may lead to Santa Fe."

The visitor bell clanged in the outer office. Kingsley glanced at the young lad who ran telegrams for Western Union. "See about that, will you, Trevor?"

Trevane collected the telegram and tossed the boy two bits. He returned to Kingsley's office and handed him the telegram.

Kingsley tore it open.

"Well it seems we have a new development. Our Cajun friend has gone missing from the Cheyenne jail."

"Missing?" Trevane and Samantha said as one.

"Walked out in the middle of the night courtesy of a hairpin."

"A hairpin?" Samantha chuckled.

"Terribly unprofessional," Kingsley said.

"So now where are we?" Trevane asked.

"On the next stage to Santa Fe," Samantha said.

Sheriff's Office
Cheyenne

Firth sat at his desk. His head ached. The coffee didn't help. The problem, how to explain to the city council how a high-profile prisoner simply got up and walked out of his jail. *He did it with a hairpin?* That's what Endicott told him. A hairpin! It was embarrassing. It was also true, as far as he could determine. The office door opened. He glanced up to misty gust from a rain spattered street and a well-dressed gentleman tailored and groomed down to the point of a graying goatee.

"Sheriff Firth?"

"I'm Collin Firth."

"Montegue Malthus, Claims Special Agent, Comprehensive Insurance Company. I believe Colonel David Crook of the Great Western Detective League wired you with reference to a visit with your prisoners."

"Ah, yes." He rose to take Malthus's hand.

"Would it be possible to interview the prisoners now?"

"Prisoner."

He wrinkled his brow. "I thought there were two."

"There were. One of them left."

"Left?"

"Opened his cell with a hairpin and walked out in the middle of the night."

"You're joking."

"I wish I were."

"Don't tell me. The box man?"

"The very one. For your purposes, though, you didn't miss much. That one kept his mouth shut. The one we still hold is our canary."

"I see. May I interview him then?"

"If it's all right with the Colonel, it's all right with me."

"Curiously effective, the relationship your Colonel has with local law enforcement the way I see it."

"We are the backbone of the league. Right this way."

He showed Malthus into the cell block. Endicott's disposition hadn't improved.

"You've got a visitor, Endicott."

He squinted into the gray gloom admitting the patter of rain on the roof. "Who are you?"

"Montegue Malthus, Comprehensive Insurance Company."

Twenty minutes later Malthus left the cell block.

"Learn anything?" Firth asked.

"Confirmed some things the Colonel reported with respect to the criminal syndicate known as *El Anillo*. He did offer some new information that might prove useful. Can you direct me to the courthouse?"

"As a matter of fact, I was just on my way to the city council woodshed over there."

"Your city council maintains a woodshed at the courthouse?"

"In a manner of speaking. They frown on high-profile prisoners checking out of jail."

Raton Pass

Cane hung on the *El Anillo* man's trail. It settled into a leisurely pace, allowing Cane to stay close without giving his presence away. The ferret seemed little concerned with the possibility he might be followed. Descending Uncle Dick's toll road to Wootton's inn, Cane expected to find the man taking a night off the trail. He reached the toll gate at dusk. He paid the lad tending the gate his twenty-five-cent toll and spotted Escobar's horse in the corral. Too bad. After the run-in they had over the bearer-bond case, the man was sure to recognize him if he were to take a room and a hot meal. Nothing for it but to ride on and camp below the inn along the Santa Fe Trail.

O'Rourke House

Denver

She found him in his room feverishly packing at midmorning.

"In again, out again, gone again, Finnigan."

"What?"

"Old Irish saying for a sailor gone to sea. Where to this time?"

"Santa Fe."

"Perhaps I should just rent you a closet. It would save you some money, and I could rent out this room to someone who might actually use it."

He paused with a smile. "You do miss me."

She clenched her fists on her hips. "Why are you so obsessed with me missing you?"

"I'm not. I'm obsessed with you."

"When you're not otherwise obsessed."

He threw up his hands and turned to his packing. "Maybe she's right after all."

"Who's right?"

"Samantha."

"Her again. Will she be going to Santa Fe?"

"Can't say. Doesn't matter. There's nothing between us."

"You say. What's she so right about this time?"

"She doesn't know which one of us is the greater fool. You for not knowing what you're missing; or me for knowing and not . . ." It took only one long stride to sweep her up in his arms. You couldn't exactly call her resistance a struggle. More like an annoyed wriggle until the kiss melted.

She gasped, holding him as tightly as he held her. "You are a thoroughly vexing man, Beau Longstreet."

"Pleasantly so, given half the chance."

"Perhaps . . . I am the fool."

"Beautifully so." He kissed her again.

"Now, about that closet: have you one available in your room?"

"I give in for a penny, and you ask for the whole of a pound."

"I'm a patient man, Maddie O'Rourke. Patient and persistent."

"I can see that." She tipped up on her toes and kissed him.

"Miss me."

"I shall consider it."

He closed his case and dashed down the stairs.

She followed with her eyes, thoroughly . . . vexed.

Stage Depot
Denver

Longstreet made it to the stage depot with little time to spare and less interest in travel than his desire to roil Maddie O'Rourke's steadfast resolve. He went straight to the counter and purchased his ticket. He turned to the passenger lounge where a smile and a scowl greeted him. Samantha met him with a light in her eye. Trevane postured a demeanor somewhat less enthused by the prospect of his joining the journey.

"On the way to Santa Fe?" Samantha teased.

Longstreet nodded a pleasant smile for Trevane's benefit.

"Whatever for?" Samantha said.

"Can't imagine. What about you?"

"Oh, the usual fool's errand filled with the false promise of opportunity."

"At least the company's improved for the trip," Longstreet said.

Trevane scowled.

"You do hold yourself in high opinion, Mr. Longstreet," Samantha said.

"You've never complained before."

"I never traveled with Trevor before."

"I see."

Trevane preened.

"All aboard!" the driver called from the door.

CHAPTER THIRTY-FOUR

Court House
Cheyenne

Rain spattered the boardwalk overhang, puddling in the ruts in the street. Gray skies rumpled in felt folds rolling over the mountains. Firth showed Malthus to the county clerk's office.

"Well, this is it. Careful will take good care of you."

The bespectacled little man behind the counter smiled.

"Careful?"

"Careful Johnson. Who else would you want for a county clerk?"

"I see."

"Careful, take good care of Mr. Malthus here. I'm off to the city council chamber."

"Good luck, Sheriff," Malthus said.

"Hope the councilmen have their sense of humor with them today."

Malthus turned to the clerk.

"How may I be of service, Mr. Malthus?"

"I believe you have some recent filings in which I am interested."

The clerk took a pad and moistened the tip of a pencil on his tongue.

"The claim filing for one Jeweled Garden, along with business organizations for"—Malthus consulted his own notes—"ah yes, for Jeweled Garden Partners and Consolidated Mining."

Moments later the clerk laid a stack of papers on the counter.

An hour later Malthus thanked the clerk and left his office only to meet the sheriff coming downstairs from the council chamber.

"How'd it go, Sheriff?"

Firth winced. "I still have my badge."

"There is that to be thankful for."

"How about you?"

"Interesting. I'll say that."

The courthouse door opened to sheets of rain pouring down beyond the boardwalk. Firth looked at the sky.

"Looks like this might keep up a spell. Care for a coffee?"

"That sounds good."

"Sarah's Café is just next door. She may even have a slice of pie to go with it. You can tell me all about your interesting findings."

Sarah kept a small, cozy restaurant with red-and-white-checked tablecloths and red napkins. Fresh, warm apple pie, as it turned out. They ordered two slices and coffee.

"So what did Careful come up with that was so interesting?"

"The road map to a plot, it appears. The claim for the Jeweled Garden mine was filed in the name of Jeweled Garden Partners, a corporation."

Firth stabbed the air with his fork. "I wondered about that Jeweled Garden. Strikes me as an odd name for a mine."

"It would be, if it were a mine. It's not. It's a garden. A garden they planted. Jeweled Garden partners issued a million shares common equity at a dollar per share. Four hundred thousand shares went to the San Francisco investors, Crocker and Leland; two hundred thousand to our friends Endicott and Duval over in your lockup. Another three hundred thousand went to New York investors and one hundred thousand to Chas. Sterling & Co."

"The Jeweler?"

"It would appear so."

"That has the ring of legitimacy to it."

"It does, doesn't it? Clever bastards, the lot of them, it would appear. Now this is where it gets even more interesting. Another three hundred thousand were issued to Golden J Investment Trust in care of Salmon Chase Bank of New York."

"Who's that?"

"That, my good sheriff, is the very question. We shall have to confirm it, of course, but I'd be willing to bet you a handsome sum we will find it a blind trust."

"Blind trust?"

"A legal instrument constructed so as to assure the anonymity of the owner."

"So we can't find out who that investor is."

"Precisely."

"So what happened to the money?"

"Proceeds from the investments were to be transferred by wire to Cheyenne Union Bank for the benefit of the account of Jeweled Garden Partners."

"Franklin Pierpont's bank. It's just up the street. I'm sure he'll recall handling sums like that. We shouldn't even get wet on the way to see him."

"I'm sure he'll recall, though I've a pretty good idea what happened next based on the third filing."

"What was that?"

"Incorporation papers for one Consolidated Mining Co."

"Never heard of it."

"Of course not. Let's go see your banker friend."

Franklin Pierpont sat at a massive, polished wood desk flanking an imposing steel vault door. Cheyenne Union Bank exuded the feeling of power and strength people sought when entrusting their money. The lobby décor reeked understated dignity. The banker fit the part in his dark suit, starched collar, and gray cravat with a gold stickpin. His austerity cracked in practiced greeting to the sheriff accompanied by a distinguished stranger. He rose.

"Sheriff Firth, welcome. How may we be of service today?"

"Franklin, may I present Montegue Malthus, Claims Special Agent for Comprehensive Insurance Company."

Malthus extended his hand and a card.

The banker shook his hand, studying the card. "Claims special agent accompanied by a sheriff. Is something amiss?"

"Perceptive," Malthus said.

"And our bank is affected?"

"We believe so. May we?" Malthus gestured toward the banker's side chairs.

"Please." They settled into their chairs.

"Now, what makes you think Cheyenne Union might assist in your investigation? It is an investigation is it not?"

"It is. Do you hold an account for Jeweled Garden Partners?"

"We do." The banker's sober expression clouded at mention of so substantial an account.

"And might you also hold an account for Consolidated Mining?"

"We do."

"And has there recently been a rather substantial amount of business transacted between the two companies? Say substantial in the amount of eight hundred thousand dollars."

"I don't know the answer to that without checking."

"Please."

He summoned with a wave a mousy little man who held the position of cashier. He relayed the question. The affirmative answer came without necessity of inspecting the account records.

"And might there have been substantial disbursements from

the Consolidated Mining Account?" Malthus said.

The cashier nodded.

"The whole of the eight hundred thousand?"

"Is there a problem?" The cashier said.

"Answer the man," Pierpont said.

"Disbursements have been made."

"By what instrument?" Malthus said.

"Cashier's drafts."

"Made out to 'cash.' "

"Why yes. How did you know?"

Pierpont looked to Firth. Firth looked to Malthus. Malthus nodded.

CHAPTER THIRTY-FIVE

Wootton's Inn
Raton Pass

The Denver stage rolled off the toll road into the hot, dusty yard at Wootton's Inn and Station. The driver hauled lines and set the brake for two lads who began unhitching the team.

"Thirty-minute meal stop," he called from the box.

Longstreet climbed down from the coach. He offered Samantha a hand she accepted. She took his arm, followed by a disgruntled Trevane. The shaded inn provided a measure of respite from the heat and dust of the trail. The dining room was all but deserted at midday but for pockets of blue shadow.

The dour proprietor known as Uncle Dick greeted them with what passed for his smile. "Roast beef and mashed is the special. What'll it be, folks?"

"Three specials," Samantha said.

"Good choice when all you've got is thirty minutes to spare. Coming right up."

Samantha cast about the room. "I'll wager they have rooms here with real beds and a bathtub to go with it. A person could stretch out her kinks and shed a layer of grime."

"We could take a break and continue on tomorrow's stage," Trevane said.

"I doubt there's anything in Santa Fe that won't keep another day," Longstreet said.

Samantha pursed her lips. "You, of course, would continue

on to press your advantage."

"Advantage? Oh, please; all the advantage would be had in lingering here with you."

"If I believed that for a moment, Beau, dearest, you'd have silver-tongued your way into my heart once again. But, alas, this is Samantha. You do remember? Of course you do. How silly of me to even question it."

"It was my suggestion," Trevane said.

She patted his cheek as the roast beef arrived. "So it was and not an altogether unpleasant thought at that."

He half smiled. "Thanks. I think."

"Pity. I shall miss your witty company," Longstreet said.

"Don't fret over it in the least, my dear. You shan't distract us from our mission so easily. Now you best eat that before it gets cold."

"Easily? I can't imagine you an easy distraction."

Trevane cut his eyes from one to the other, trying to shake the feeling he was always one step behind.

Samantha smiled at her first bite of roast beef. She had them both coming and going. It amused her.

Stage Depot
Santa Fe

The coach lurched to a stop. Trevane piled out, offering a hand to Samantha before Longstreet could lead her away. The driver unloaded the baggage boot, setting their bags on the boardwalk. Trevane collected his bag and Samantha's. He started up Palace toward Washington and the Capitol Plaza Hotel. Samantha glanced over her shoulder.

"Are you coming?"

"You seem in good hands. I'll be along."

She feigned a pout and followed Trevane.

Cane stepped out of the shadows of the depot porch. "Actually, you won't be along."

"We're not staying at the Capitol?"

"Too obvious. The ring knows everything that goes on in this town. They'll spot our Pinkerton friends before the ink is dry on the register."

"So where are we staying?"

"You'll see."

"I'm sure." He picked up his bag and followed Cane down Palace to Grant.

Cane turned in under a signboard that read Regal Oriental. Regal hardly suited the seedy saloon and hotel.

Longstreet glanced around a wrinkled nose. "Do I need to check in?"

"Took care of that."

They climbed a decrepit flight of stairs to a balcony overlooking the saloon, lined with what would be cribs for soiled doves in such establishments. More than a few probably were. Cane led them down a dark corridor toward the back of the building. He admitted them to a spare, dirty room with a bed, lamp stand, cracked window, and coat tree.

"Spared no expense on this place, I see." Longstreet dropped his bag. The bed sagged. "Who gets the bed?"

"Won't need it. We'll be workin'."

"So where did our boy go?"

"Don't know. He disappeared before I hit town."

"So here we sit in this dump with nothing to show for it but a stone-cold trail."

"We'll ask around. Sooner or later we find them, or they find us."

"If they're going to find us anyway, why don't we have them find us comfortably ensconced at the Plaza?"

"Because if they find our Pinkerton friends first, there's a chance we find them before they find us."

"Now there's a good bit of tortured logic."

"Feel tortured if you must. This way keeps our options open. I'll do the askin' while you watch our back."

"You think that's how it plays out?"

"Count on it."

"If you're right about the Plaza, maybe the backs we should watch are our Pinkerton friends."

A light flickered in Cane's eye. "You know, Longstreet, you just might earn your keep yet."

CHAPTER THIRTY-SIX

Capitol Plaza Hotel

Samantha and Trevane entered the spacious, opulent lobby. They crossed to the reception desk and signed the register.

"Where do we begin?" Trevane said.

"I don't know about you, but I'm beginning with a bath and a hot meal I don't have to bolt down in thirty minutes or less. Past that, I suppose we ask around."

"You order your bath. I'll get these bags settled and start asking around. What time should I meet you for dinner, or are you hoping for a better offer from Longstreet?"

She lifted her chin with a mischievous smile. "Not an altogether unpleasant notion."

"Which?"

"Say, six." She swept up the stairs, leaving him to carry her bag.

Women. Trevane turned off Washington onto Palace retracing his steps to the stage depot and the promise of seedier saloons beyond. *Who knew what they were thinking most of the time?* In the case of Samantha Maples the conundrum seemed doubly confounding. He couldn't escape the feeling she toyed with him. It amused her. He wasn't amused. At least not by her flirtations with the big southerner. The man was a bother to have around. It got in the way of his own . . . amusement.

185

★　★　★　★　★

Cane and Longstreet sat on a cigar store bench on the corner of Palace and Washington where they could observe the Capitol Plaza Hotel entrance. Smoke and Longstreet's newly rented livery mount stood quiet at a hitch rack east of Palace on Washington.

"Lookee yonder." Cane lifted his chin into the slanting afternoon light. "Here comes one of them backs we're watchin'. Where do you suppose he's headed?"

"Your guess is as good as mine."

"Best follow him."

"You go. I'll keep a lookout here."

"You watch her whilst I watch him. I mighta guessed."

"Proof positive."

"Proof of what?"

"Your guess is as good as mine."

Cane ambled off behind the unsuspecting Trevane, following along from the other side of the street a block to the rear.

Trevane paused on the corner of Palace and Grant. A chipped painted sign over a squat adobe a short walk down the block to the west proclaimed *El Lobo.* The faded picture of a lone wolf howled at a moon silvered in weathered wood. It looked like as good a place as any to start. He adjusted his shoulder rig to a comfortable position under his coat and ambled down the block to the batwings.

Inside the cantina, little more moved than dust motes floating in narrow shafts of window light. He slipped inside, letting his eyes adjust. The bar beckoned. His eyes adjusted to a reason to choose a vacant table in back instead. He'd no more than settled in his chair when she came to his side. Dark eyes smoldered under a tossed curtain of long, black hair. Dark copper swelled a simple peasant blouse. A multicolored skirt hugged rounded hips, falling to bare feet on the dirt floor.

"What is it *señor* wishes?"

"Tequila. Bring a glass for yourself if you like."

She turned to the bar in a swirl. She returned with two glasses and a bottle. She took a seat beside him and poured. She lifted her glass.

"*Salud.*"

"I make it a practice never to drink with a beautiful woman without knowing her name."

"Maria."

"Maria, *salud.*"

They tossed off their drinks. She poured.

"What brings *señor* to Santa Fe?"

"I search."

She laughed deep and throaty. "Don't we all? What is it you search for?"

"Information." He slid a gold double eagle across the table.

She eyed it. "All this for information?"

"Perhaps more."

She lifted a brow. He could feel her heat. She smelled of sandalwood. *Perhaps the information could wait.*

"What is this information that is worth golden eagles?"

"I wish to find someone."

She shrugged. "Many men come to *El Lobo.*"

"This man is *El Anillo.*"

Her eyes shot round and white. She crossed herself. "*Señor* does not have enough golden eagles to make that bird sing."

She tossed off her drink and left him the bottle.

Cane found Longstreet where he'd left him and took his place on the bench as they watched Trevane return to the hotel.

"Well?" Longstreet said.

"He went to a cantina not far from our hotel. I chanced a

look inside. He had a drink with a girl."

"A girl. I wonder if Samantha knows."

Cane shook his head. "He didn't stay long enough for her to be concerned. Does Maddie know you're that obsessed with the Maples woman?"

"Obsessed? Samantha? Hardly. We had our time before Maddie came along, if you must know. Assuming Maddie has . . . never mind. What did you make of it?"

"Make of what?"

"Trevane and the girl."

"He either got what he wanted or he didn't."

"Well that about covers the possibilities. Now that we've got that behind us, where do we go from here?"

"There," Cane said.

A dark rider rounded the corner from Washington in the lengthening shadows of sunset. The big black Cajun rode south on Palace at a jog.

CHAPTER THIRTY-SEVEN

Samantha stretched languid in a tub scented with lilac soap floating in puddles of bubbles. Her head rested on a rolled towel draped over the rim. Trail dust and ache drained away in warm, soapy comfort. Her eyes drooped, half lidded. A knock sounded at the door.

"Who is it?"

"Trevor. We need to talk."

"I'm taking a bath."

"I don't mind."

"I'm sure you don't. Now be a good boy and run along to the salon. I'll meet you there directly." She sat up. Nowhere near finished with her relaxation. She picked up the towel and rose, draining rivulets on soap suds. She resigned to the comforts of a towel dry and a clean change of clothes. She caught her reflection in the mirror over a small dresser. Beau Longstreet crossed her mind's eye. Trevor waited.

Duval trotted down Palace to Grant. He swung west in lengthening blue shadows. The sign out front of a sprawling two-story adobe read *Rosa's*. He drew rein and stepped down. He tied his horse at the rail and entered a candlelit reception hall. An attractive older woman who still did justice to her daring gown smiled.

"Welcome to *Rosa's, señor*. How may we be of service?"

"I am looking for a friend. His name is Escobar."

Her brows lifted. "*Senor* Escobar is not here."

"I trust he will find out I am."

"*Si.*"

"I need a room while I wait for him."

"Of course."

"I have a horse outside."

"Paco will see to it. Do you wish someone to see to your other needs?"

He nodded. "After a bath to clean up from the trail."

"Both can be arranged." She clapped once. A dark-eyed girl of exquisite beauty appeared. "Collette, show *Señor . . .*"

"Duval."

"Show *Señor* Duval to the bath and your room. He may be with us a few days."

"The rate?"

"Twenty dollars a day."

He handed Rosa two double eagles and followed the girl.

Cane signaled a halt at their hotel.

"That's his horse up yonder."

"It is."

They stepped down and tied up.

"Let's have a look," Cane said. He led the way up the block, close enough to read the sign. Just then a Mexican boy came out to the rail. He collected the horse and led him into the alley toward the back of the imposing adobe.

"Looks like he's fixin' to stay a spell," Longstreet said.

"Does."

They walked back up the street to the hotel porch. "Get some shut-eye. I'll take first watch," Longstreet said.

"I'll put Smoke up 'til I spell you." He led the gray in back to the stable.

Longstreet stuck his head into the hotel doorway and signaled

the bartender for a bottle. He settled into a chair on the porch
with a view of Rosa's front door.

She found Trevane in the dimly lit salon. Islands of candlelight
flickered on polished dark-wood tabletops as she crossed the
room. A bottle and glasses waited. He rose to hold her chair.

"Lavender, my favorite."

"I'm sure. Now, what's so bloody important a girl can't
indulge in a civilized bath?"

"You didn't have to get out."

"Please."

He poured drinks and passed hers across the table.

"Chances of picking up information on *El Anillo* are not
good."

"How can you possibly be sure so soon? You weren't gone
long enough for a proper bath."

"Mention the name and you get two reactions. Fear and
'There's not enough money.' "

"Fear is no surprise. Not enough money to buy information
is a problem."

"So, I don't know how we pick up a trail, unless we follow
Longstreet. Something brought him down here."

"That may be a problem, too."

"Why?"

"He's not registered here. He could be anywhere."

"You checked?"

She returned his clipped answer with a smile. "Bother you?"
She lifted her glass and took a smooth swallow.

"Would it matter if it did?"

"It might."

"Then it does."

She patted his cheek. "Buy a girl some supper and we'll see."

"See what?"

191

"If it matters."

Morning light spilled over the sill, seeping through gauzy lace curtains. Samantha's eyes fluttered open. Trevane snored softly. *He might not be Beau Longstreet, but all things considered . . .* She let her thoughts drift over the evening just passed.

All right, she brought her attention back to the matter at hand. They'd hit a dead end. Longstreet and Cane could be anywhere. They had a trail. She and Trevor had . . . well, she and Trevor—She bolted up in bed.

"That's it."

Trevane rolled over. "It is?"

"It is."

"It is what?"

"Where we go from here."

"I've got a pretty good idea."

"Not that. Where we go to find *El Anillo.*"

"I'm listening."

"We start an inquiry after the Cajun."

"The Cajun. He could be anywhere. What makes you think he's here?"

"I have no idea."

"Then why start an inquiry?"

"Look, he's either here or he's not. If he's here, they'll know it. If he's not here, they'll wonder why we're looking for him here. Either way, it'll feel too close for comfort. They'll find us."

"If they find us we better have our backs."

"Come on." She threw back the covers.

He caught her arm.

She glanced over her shoulder.

"I got your back."

All things considered . . .

CHAPTER THIRTY-EIGHT

Hacienda Carnicero

Escobar knocked at the library door.

"*¡Entrar en!*"

Don Victor sat at his desk, bathed in late-afternoon light, the desk top piled high in twenty-dollar gold certificates. "What have you learned?"

"Much. Much that is not good."

The Don tore himself away from the fruits of his erstwhile diamond mine. "Speak."

"Pinkerton captured the geologist and the Cajun."

"What did they learn?"

"The Cajun held his tongue."

"*Bien.* The geologist?"

"Did not."

"*Muerte.*"

"*Sí, Patrón.*" Endicott's death sentence served.

"There is more. The Cajun escaped."

"Then we are done with him as planned."

"Perhaps, but we are not rid of him. Rosa sends word. A man calling himself Duval is a guest in her house. He wishes to speak with us."

"Unfortunate choice. Do you suppose he left a trail to us?"

The ferret shrugged. "Anything is possible."

"I think you should see to his need."

"*Sí, Patrón.*"

Capitol Plaza Hotel

Samantha lavished a most fetching and satisfied smile on the scarecrow clerk with a roving eye at the registration desk.

"I would like to leave a message for a guest, a Monsieur Duval."

The clerk ran a bony finger down the guest registration. "I'm sorry, madam, we have no one registered here by that name."

"A black man, Cajun, I think. Are you sure?"

"Quite sure."

"I would have sworn he'd stay here."

"Perhaps he has yet to arrive. Is there a message you wish me to give him should he check in?"

She shook her head. "No, no. It must be a surprise." She turned on her heel and crossed the polished lobby to the waiting Trevane. The clerk followed the sway of her hips, curious.

Rosa's

Collette straddled Duval's supine frame, the room low lit in candlelight from the bedside table. For all her petite delicacy she possessed strong hands and firm fingers she applied expertly to knotted muscles in his thick neck and broad, ebony back. She made small curiosity of the lash scars in his flesh but gave them no more than a passing glance at that. All in all, she made the care he received at Rosa's worth every penny of the exorbitant price. A knock sounded at the door.

"What is it?" he said.

"A message for *Señor* Duval."

"Under the door. Be a dear and fetch that for me."

She slipped off his back and padded across the room, a tawny slip of a sylph. She picked up the piece of paper and returned to the bed. She laid the note beside him, crawled astride his back, and resumed her ministrations. He unfolded the note and read. It summoned him to an old adobe in the hills east of town.

"Tell Paco I need my horse."

"You are leaving?" She pulled a pretty pout.

He rolled over, holding her eyes. "Presently."

She smiled.

Regal Oriental Hotel

A scrawny lad in a straw sombrero led the big bay through the alley from the stable in back of Rosa's. Cane rocked his tipped-back chair forward and stepped to the lobby door. He motioned the sleepy-eyed desk clerk awake. The man crossed the dingy lobby. Cane tossed him a silver dollar.

"Tell Mr. Longstreet to saddle his horse and meet me out front, now."

The clerk sensed urgency, making a half-hearted attempt to hurry up the stairs. Minutes later Longstreet led his horse up the alley. He found Cane holding Smoke out of sight at the mouth of the alley.

"What's up?"

Cane lifted his chin up the street. The bay stood quietly at Rosa's hitch rack. "They brought his horse out a few minutes ago. Looks like he's fixin' to head off somewhere."

Time passed, gathering shadows as daylight faded toward evening. Down the street the door to Rosa's opened. The Cajun appeared in the doorway framed in lamplight. A slip of a girl in a gauzy gown accompanied him. She tipped up on her toes and kissed him. He gave her an affectionate squeeze and turned to his horse.

"Looks like our boy had a fine time," Longstreet said.

Duval stepped into the saddle with a wave to the girl silhouetted in the doorway and swung east.

"He's coming this way," Cane said, backing Smoke into the shadows.

Duval jogged east on Grant, swinging north on Palace. Cane stepped into his saddle and squeezed up a lope along Grant.

Longstreet reined in on his flank.

Duval wheeled east on Washington trailing puffs of dun dust as he headed into the hills northeast of town.

The Cajun left a trail plain enough even in dwindling light. Cane had little difficulty following it over rolling hills covered in sage and creosote bush. A half moon rose with nightfall. The trail climbed into the hills, bearing north, weaving its way up a narrow defile to a small level pause in the hillside. Cane signaled a halt.

Ahead, an old adobe stood ghost-like by the light of the moon. The hobbled bay browsed in the yard. A faint light glowed in one window.

Longstreet leaned forward, resting his hands on the saddle horn. "Do we go in and take him?"

Cane cut his eyes to him. "You of all people."

"Me. What?"

"Do you suppose he left a whore's warm bed to ride out here by himself? He's waiting for someone. Someone we're likely to find interesting." He nodded to a stand of white oak at the northwest edge of the plateau. "We'll hole up there and see what develops."

He eased Smoke around the side of the hill, keeping out of sight. They picketed the horses in the trees and resumed their watch.

CHAPTER THIRTY-NINE

Gray light burst into spears of morning sun. The fiery orb climbed the morning sky to full light. The adobe stood quiet other than the Cajun pausing to relieve himself. Longstreet brushed away a fly.

"What the hell are we waiting for?"

Cane half lifted lids under his tilted-down hat brim. "He came out here for a reason."

"So far all he's managed to do is take a piss."

"Patience, my friend. Good things come to those who wait."

"Says who?"

"The wise."

"Wise my ass." He waved the fly away again.

Time passed. The sun inched its way toward midday. A dark rider crested the plateau from the south amid heat shimmers.

"Check this."

Cane pushed up his hat brim. They watched him ride in, high-stepping, flashy black in broad-pommel Mexican tack. A thin man in a wide-brimmed sombrero trailing a wisp of cigar smoke stepped down.

"Well, well, look who's here," Cane said.

The ferret glanced around to confirm he was alone. He ducked into the adobe.

Escobar's sudden appearance startled Duval. The ferret swept the gloom. *Alone.* Bien. His eyes adjusted to the dim light.

"Very clever," he said.

"Clever?"

"The hairpin."

"Cracker-box jail. I never go anywhere without one."

"What brings you back to us?"

"I need to get out of the country."

Escobar nodded. "We suspected as much. Don Victor agrees."

"I need money."

"You were paid for your work, were you not?"

"You don't get to keep it when you are arrested."

He shook his head. "That is unfortunate."

"Most unfortunate."

"And how is this our concern?"

"It is in our mutual interest for me to get out of the country. If I am apprehended again, my hairpin may not suffice for my freedom."

"That too would be unfortunate. I must speak with the Don."

Escobar turned to go.

"Damn quiet in there," Longstreet said.

"Too quiet."

"Should we take them both?"

Cane shook his head. "How long did we hold the Mexican the last time we collared him?"

Cane was right. *El Anillo* had him out on bond before they got back to the office. Out on a bond, he jumped into thin air without second thought.

Two quick shots rang out. Longstreet cut his eyes to Cane. Escobar left the adobe, holstering a smoking gun. He collected his horse and wheeled away to the southeast.

"Now we're getting somewhere," Cane said.

"We are?"

"We are." He collected Smoke and swung into the saddle.

Longstreet followed. "What about him?" He thumbed the adobe.

"He ain't goin' anywhere. Time enough to bury him later." He squeezed up a lope along the ferret's dusty trail.

Hacienda Carnicero

The Mexican laid down a clean trail with no apparent concern for being followed. He skirted Santa Fe continuing south. Something on the order of an hour from Santa Fe, the trail climbed into hill country before spilling out onto a broad mesa. Cane drew rein at the crest. The Mexican rode on toward a walled *hacienda* set on a low rise near the center of the plateau.

"Nobody gets close to that without bein' noticed," Longstreet said.

Cane stepped down. "We'll ride on in for a closer look after dark."

They ground-tied the horses and let the day play out into evening.

Don Victor savored a fine agave tequila with an aromatic cigar on his private veranda alone with the sunset. Approaching boot heels tatted the tiles. He expected the news.

"*Buena noches, Patrón.*"

"You have seen to our friend?"

"He is no longer in need of our assistance."

"*Bueno.*"

"We have a report from one of our people. Pinkerton agents inquired after him at the Capitol Plaza."

The Don released a cloud of fragrant smoke. A small muscle bunched in his jaw. He slacked it with a swallow of tequila. "How many?"

"Two. A man and a woman, as best we know."

"A woman?"

"*Sí.*"

"Gringos." He shook his head. "Eliminate them."

"Perhaps they will find nothing and go away. If we kill them, more will come."

"The Pinkerton hunt for money. They profit little from death. Eliminate them."

"Sí, Patrón."

They rode in under cloud-covered darkness. The walled *hacienda* loomed a black fortress set atop its perch on the plain. Cane led the way, circling east to the north and west, returning to the gated front façade. Lighted windows glowed from the second floor visible above the wall. The dwelling set back against the back wall, set off from the gate by what must be a broad plaza. Cane knit his brows and scratched the stubble on his chin.

"Gonna take some to crack that box."

"Some what?"

"Not sure yet. Need to think on it. C'mon, let's get off this rock and outta sight. See if morning sheds light on the problem."

"Morning dew turns the walls to gingerbread?" Longstreet said.

"Likely it'll take stronger than dew."

The heat of the day faded to cooler evening. Still hot with pain and fever. He'd managed a little water. He couldn't stay here. He needed attention or surely he would die. Die, that was the plan. This once he vowed they would come up short. In time he would balance accounts, but, for now, he needed to survive.

He crawled to the adobe door. His horse cropped quietly in his hobbles, nearby. Could he mount? It started with standing. He used his left arm to inch himself up the doorframe. His right side hung useless. Agony poured sweat in his eyes. The world behind his eyes spun unsteadily. He took a painful breath to clear his head. He put a boot forward. His knee wobbled but held. Another. Then another. He used pain to stay conscious. Step by step, the horse loomed closer, swimming in twilight.

He gathered the reins and loosed the hobbles, gasping for breath. He nearly swooned, slipping into darkness. He refused. His left hand caught the saddle horn. He paused to clear his head. Stirrup. Left toe. He stabbed and missed. Stabbed again. Caught purchase and hauled himself up.

He nudged the way south.

Rosa's

The dark rider slumped over his horse's neck plodded down the alley to the stable yard. The horse turned its nose to the scent of grain at the stable door. The reins dropped to the ground. The rider slipped down and stumbled inside, collapsing on a pile of straw.

Two dark eyes rounded white in low light at the sight of him. A dark hand reached out to the boy offering a silver dollar.

"Collette." Barely whispered.

Paco ran.

Darkness closed in.

Someone knelt at his side. Strong fingers.

Hacienda Carnicero

They cold-camped off the trail below the crest of the mesa. Cane was up with the sun, studying the wall through a tarnished brass field glass.

"The view improve any from here?" Longstreet said.

No answer.

"Wait a minute. Somethin's up."

"What?"

Cane handed him the glass. He picked out four heavily armed riders headed their way. "One in the lead looks like Escobar."

"It does."

"Busy boy. What do you suppose they're up to this time?"
Cane shrugged. "One way to find out. Mount up."

CHAPTER FORTY

Santa Fe

Escobar and his men drew rein on the outskirts of town. There they split into pairs. Cane and Longstreet watched the first pair ride off into town.

"What do you make of it," Longstreet asked.

"Don't draw no attention that way."

"Where do you suppose they're headed?"

"You got the questions, Beau. It's the answers that's troublesome. I figure we follow the ferret we'll find out soon enough."

Minutes later Escobar and the last man rode into town.

Samantha and Trevane canvassed merchants and business establishments along Palace carrying out their erstwhile enquiry into the whereabouts of the Cajun known as Duval. By the afternoon of the second day they'd about exhausted the possibilities. They paused to rest on a bench outside a cigar store.

"He's either not here or in serious hiding," Trevane said.

"Not important. By now everyone in town knows we're looking for him, which means our friends know or soon will."

"You think that will flush them into the open?"

She nodded.

"Be careful what you wish for. The informant we found in that graveyard in Denver paid a dear price for crossing this bunch."

"Nervous, love?"

"Love doesn't make me nervous. Knives do."

"What have we here?"

A lone rider wheeled off Palace onto Lincoln bound for the government corral. He turned into the low, walled quadrangle and stepped down in the dusty yard. He led his horse into the stable and disappeared in dark shadow inside.

"Our ferret-faced friend. Come on." Samantha set off across Palace for Lincoln.

Trevane swallowed his second thoughts, checked his shoulder rig, and followed along.

By the time they reached the stable yard, there was no sign of the Mexican. Shadows crept across the quadrangle from the darkened stable doors.

"We just going to wander on in there without knowing what we're up against?" Trevane said.

"You are a nervous Nellie. It's one scrawny little Mexican."

"Suppose he's meeting some other not-so-scrawny Mexicans in there."

"Then we just came by to rent horses."

"You expect them to believe that? You said yourself they probably know we're here."

She bit her lip.

"You heeled?" Trevane said.

"Of course."

"Then I'll go in. You back me."

"Why, Trevor dear, I had no idea you were so gallant."

"Fool for a pretty face."

"I'm flattered."

"More important, you're heeled."

They paused to listen at the stable door. Silence. Trevor stepped into the shadows and paused, allowing his eyes to adjust to dim light. A straw-strewn dirt floor stretched into dim confines between two rows of stalls, faintly lit by chinks and cracks in the old stable timbers. Horse sounds and smells muted any sense of danger. He drew his pistol and held it in his pocket out of sight. He started down the aisle between the stalls. A blinding flash of white light flared to black before his eyes. He crumpled to the dirt floor like a felled tree.

"Trevor?"

A gun pressed to her back. An iron grip froze the gun hand in her purse.

"Inside," frijole breath said.

"Looks like Samantha and Trevane," Longstreet said.

"Looks more like trouble. Come on." Cane led out along the corral wall to the back of the stable and stepped down.

"You take the back, Beau. When the *hombre* with the gun on Samantha goes down, the ball goes up."

"Got it."

Her assailant snatched her gun and shoved her inside the stable with the barrel of his. She stepped around the fallen Trevane. Two other shadows appeared in the aisle at the back of the stable, guns drawn. They wore sombreros and shirtwaist jackets. The scrawny fourth stepped out of a stall. His tiny eyes glittered black as they groped her with intent.

"You search for the Cajun Duval. Why?"

"He escaped jail."

"Careless of the jailer, no?"

"What's it to you?"

"Our interests reach far. The Cajun is not here."

"Was he?"

"I ask the questions."

"Ach . . ." The gunman at Samantha's back dropped his gun, clutching a blade protruding from his throat as he dropped to his knees choking on blood.

Escobar cut his eyes to the stable door as shots rang out behind him. He ducked into a stall.

Muzzle flashes bloomed in the shadows as Longstreet exchanged shots with the two *pistoleros* at the far end of the aisle. The stable fogged in powder smoke.

Samantha ducked into the nearest stall, dragging Trevane out of the line of fire by his boots.

Escobar wheeled his horse out of its stall, rolled over the side of his saddle, and galloped out the stable door.

Cane fired futilely at the fleeing killer, his target an empty saddle.

Longstreet cut loose a star burst from the rear stable door. One of the gunmen at the back of the stable fell. The other turned on Cane's back. His shot whined wild. Cane spun to a knee, leveled his aim on the silhouette, and fired. The gunman slumped forward, his gun discharging harmlessly into the dirt floor.

Longstreet toed the bodies of both downed gunmen as he passed up the aisle. Samantha stepped out of her stall.

"Don't know if I've ever been this happy to see you, Beau."

"You really should be more careful of the company you keep."

Cane stepped into the gloom from the bright stable yard. He retrieved his blade from the throat of the third gunman. "No more trouble from this one."

"What about the one who got away?" Samantha said.

"We know where he's headed," Longstreet said.

"We do?"

Longstreet smiled.

Trevane groaned and sat up.

"You all right?" Samantha said.

"What happened?"

"You missed all the fun thanks to Briscoe and Beau here."

Beau. Trevane minded his headache.

Dinner was the least they could do. Samantha insisted. Trevane put his bruised ego and aching head to bed. The hotel dining room was subdued, with a handful of diners scattered among the tables. Samantha, Longstreet, and Cane sat at a candlelit table enjoying steaks and a fine bottle of Bordeaux.

"So, how did you manage to get yourself into that little fix this afternoon?" Longstreet said.

"Unlike some"—she lifted a brow to Cane—"we didn't have a trail when we got to town. We made ourselves visible by conducting a search for Duval. He escaped from jail, you know."

"We know."

"We figured even if he wasn't here, the suggestion of a search would be enough to flush out our friends. It did. We should have anticipated an ambush. How did you happen to show up when you did? Not that a girl isn't grateful."

"We followed your friends when they came looking for you. We didn't know you were the target, but we saw they were laying an ambush plain enough."

"So that leaves us with a few loose ends—Duval, Escobar, and whoever they all work for."

"Duval ain't no loose end," Cane said around a bite of steak.

"You know where he is?"

"Old adobe in the hills northeast of town."

"Why haven't you picked him up?"

"Body ain't goin' nowhere."

"Oh."

Cane wiped his moustache on a napkin. "Mighty fine supper, Miss Samantha. My thanks."

"The thanks are all mine. If it hadn't been for you two, Trevor and I might have joined Duval in that old adobe. Now if we can only figure out who these people work for."

"On that thought, I got some figurin' of my own to do. See you in the morning, Beau." Cane pushed back his chair with a nod to Samantha and left them to finish the wine.

Longstreet topped off their glasses.

"You know, don't you?" Samantha said.

"Know what?"

"Who they work for."

"We're workin' on it."

"We could work out an exchange."

"What have you got?"

She shrugged, fluttered a lash. "Give it a little time. I'm sure something will come up."

"You talk like that, you'll give your partner another headache."

"Be serious."

"I am."

"Serious about Maddie O'Rourke."

"I never said that."

"You don't have to. Women know these things."

"You got us figured comin' and goin'."

"Of course. It's a law of nature."

Longstreet threw up his hands in mock surrender.

Rosa's

Candle light flickered silhouettes on the wall. She sat beside him on the bed wiping his fevered brow with a cool, damp cloth. He'd lapsed in and out of consciousness since the previous evening when she and the boy managed to get him to her room. She'd pieced the story together from his ravings. For a second silver dollar, Paco agreed the man was dead. What Rosa could deny knowing needed no further discussion. She bore the risk, and she would not expose herself. God willing, he would live. Anger, it seemed, made a strong life force in him.

CHAPTER FORTY-ONE

Shady Grove

His head bobbed. Pauses between thoughts lengthened. I waited patiently. The vigor that charged his wit and bearing even confined to his chair muted. I felt unease for him. A coughing fit roused him. He glanced around as though reestablishing himself among the conscious.

"Oh, Robert. Sorry. I seem to have nodded off there. Where were we?"

"I think we're about done for the day."

"Ah, no, I recall now. I received a report from Malthus on his findings in Cheyenne. The full extent of the plot was falling into place. We would have a formidable case against the mastermind and perpetrators should Cane and Longstreet be successful in apprehending those responsible."

I consulted my notes. "Eight hundred thousand dollars is an astounding sum."

"It is. The drafts, though made out to cash, told us something more. Duval and Endicott were taken with one-hundred-thousand-dollar drafts each. We had to conclude the five-hundred-thousand-dollar draft rode south with the ferret, while the remaining draft disappeared with the mysterious counselor. What happened to him, who could say? The encouraging development I reported to Malthus is that Cane and Longstreet were most assuredly hot on the trial of the largest share of the take."

He broke down in a fit of coughing once more.

As if on cue, Penney entered the solarium. He nodded off again.

"He seems tired," I said.

"He sleeps quite a lot."

"How's he doing?"

Her eyes softened in concern. She shook her head.

"I don't care for the sound of that."

"It's life, Robert. It comes for all of us in time."

I watched as she wheeled him away, with the realization he'd forgotten to ask for his weekly whiskey. I shook my head. Penney was right, of course. I needed to set aside my petty concerns for the fact I might lose the benefit of his stories. These last years provided a rare glimpse into the past. I should count myself fortunate for having had the opportunity to look through that window. I closed my notebook, pocketed it along with my pencil, and departed through reception.

Outside I took in a lungful of fresh air. I let the sun wash my face in warmth and started down the walk for home. It was more than his stories, of course. I . . . we owed the Colonel a great deal. I smiled at the memory of his introduction to Penny. My embarrassment at having my reticence exposed. Her obvious amusement at my discomfort. That, of course, had only been the beginning of his teasing. He delighted in our discomfort whenever and for whatever reason he found himself able to inflict it. I realized I would miss it. *Not now. Not yet. Please.*

The following Saturday he seemed more his irascible old self. He growled I was late, which, of course, I wasn't. As soon as Penny was out of hearing he scolded me for leaving him without his daily dram for the whole of a week. I allowed as how we both must have forgotten. Whereupon he admonished me to never let it happen again. Finally, he settled down to the purpose at hand.

"Now, where were we?"

I consulted my notes. "Cane had gone off to do some figuring."

"Ah, yes." He smiled far away. "You do recall Cane's mastery of explosives."

I'd forgotten but nodded appropriately.

"As a matter of some surprise, the morning found Longstreet where he belonged, in their room."

Regal Oriental Hotel
Santa Fe

Cane nudged Longstreet with the toe of his boot. Gray predawn light colored the room.

"What?"

"Can't sleep the day away. We got work to do."

"Day? What day?"

"The one gettin' started."

Longstreet sat up, stretched, and rubbed his eyes. "So, what's on that fertile mind of yours this early?"

"Been thinking about cracking a box."

"The *El Anillo hacienda*?"

"That's the one."

"How do you propose we go about doing that?"

"I haven't worked out all the details yet. I have a strategy in mind. We start with breakfast. Then we pick up some supplies and ride out there for a look-see. Now get dressed. I'll meet you in the café next door."

Longstreet climbed out of bed. He poured water in the wash basin and splashed it in his face. Samantha and Maddie faced off behind his eyelids. The greater fool came to mind, followed by a hankering for bacon, biscuits, and eggs topped off with a strong measure of coffee to go with it.

Hacienda Carnicero

Morning sun brightened the black-and-white-tiled veranda at the back of the hacienda. Bougainvillea scented the soft, warm breeze. Don Victor blotted *huevos rancheros* with a bit of tortilla. He washed it down with a swallow of coffee.

"Pardon, excellency."

The Don glanced up. He waved Escobar to a chair across the small table where he took his breakfast. "Coffee?"

"*Sí. Gracias.*" He poured.

"The Pinkertons, they are no longer a problem?"

The ferret cast his eyes down and shook his head. "We had them. Two *hombres* surprised us. Juan and Jose were killed in the shootout. Pedro took a knife. I was fortunate to escape."

The small muscle bunched in the Don's jaw. A cord knotted in his neck. "Who are these *hombres*?"

"I cannot be sure. It was dark. One might be the man who arrested me in El Paso last year. I heard only his voice."

"What would they be doing here?"

Escobar shrugged. "Same as the Pinkertons?"

"Hmm."

"I could take more men and eliminate all of them."

Don Victor picked up his plate and threw it against the veranda wall, shattering it in a spatter of egg and a bloody smear of pepper sauce. "No. First the Pinkertons, now other law men have come. The ones who captured the red-headed thief. Three men died there. Now, three more. All this is bungled enough. We must eliminate all of them, but how?"

Escobar sat silent staring at his coffee. The Don could be deadly, simmering in a killing rage.

"The Pinkertons." He stabbed the air with a thick forefinger. "One is a woman, no?"

"*Sí,* excellency."

"Bring her to me. The others will follow. We can deal with

212

them here, away from prying eyes in Santa Fe."

Escobar bobbed his head, scraped back his chair, and hurried off, away from the brooding storm.

Santa Fe

It looked like a typical order for trail supplies until Cane got to the end of the list—a dozen sticks of dynamite, cord fuse, and twine. Longstreet watched the clerk gingerly pack the explosives.

"What are you planning to do with that?"

"Crack a box."

"Some box."

"It is."

"No soup?"

"Too dangerous."

CHAPTER FORTY-TWO

Santa Fe

Escobar rode into town stirrup to stirrup with three heavily armed men, trailing a spare horse. He drew rein at the Capitol Plaza Hotel rail. His *compadres* rode on to wheel around back to the stable yard. The ferret stepped down, looped a rein, and mounted the entry veranda. He paused in the shade to light a cheroot, covering the street with his gaze. Satisfied all appeared quiet, he stepped into the lobby. He swept the room, allowing his eyes to adjust to a warm sepia glow. He made eye contact with the pomade-slicked desk clerk wearing garters on his sleeves. He crossed to registration.

"Hermosa mujer."

The clerk spun the register. He pointed a cracked nail to a room number. Escobar nodded and climbed the stairs. He stole down the muted second-floor hall to the door to the stable yard. He signaled his men. Two of them dismounted and climbed the stairs to join him. He led the way to room two-eleven. His men flattened on either side of the door. He knocked.

"Who is it?"

"Telegram."

Light footfalls. The door opened. Samantha's eyes went wide. Escobar grabbed her, pinning her arms as he clamped a hand to her mouth, dragging her into the room. His men bound her wrists, gagged her, and covered her head with a hood.

Escobar checked the hall. All quiet, he motioned his men

back down the hall to the stable yard. They threw her up on the spare horse and tied her ankles to the stirrups. Mounted, they led her north out of town, avoiding the heavily traveled Washington and Palace Streets.

Escobar let himself back into the hotel through the back door. He made his way down the hall to the lobby. He crossed to the front entrance as casually as any guest. He retrieved his horse, swung into the saddle, and wheeled away to the north out of town. He rejoined his men clear of town and circled southeast to the *hacienda*.

Hacienda Carnicero

"Riders comin'." Longstreet perched on the wall of an arroyo, below the mesa crest, west of the trail from town. Cane scrambled up the rocks from their concealed campsite. Dust sign curled up the trail, growing closer. The riders climbed into view—Escobar, three armed men, and one hooded captive, wearing a skirt. Longstreet cut his eyes to Cane.

"Who do you suppose that is?"

Cane shrugged.

"I got a bad feeling," Longstreet said.

"You'd be the one to know."

The riders drew rein at the gates. Moments later the gates swung open. They passed into a broad plaza. The gates closed.

"Don't just ride in there," Longstreet said.

"Nope."

"So how we gonna get in there?"

"Workin' on it."

"Work fast. I got a hunch the woman in that hood is gonna need help."

She bit one of her captors. Kneed another in the groin. Poked the ferret in the eye and wound up bound to a chair in a damp, dark storeroom of some kind. She worked her wrists raw on the bindings and her brain to a frazzle with wondering what these people could possibly want with her and what might become of her for it. She didn't like the second question, remembering Trevane's account of the informant in the cemetery. Well, they hadn't killed her yet.

Footfalls sounded on the stone floor beyond the thick wooden door to her makeshift cell. Keys jangled. The lock clicked. Hinges complained at the appearance of a shaft of lamplight. She shut her eyes against the glare. Her vision cleared.

Thick from his comforts, his features remained chiseled, swarthy and handsome with a cruel turn at the mouth. Perfectly trimmed moustache, beard, and white hair. He might have been taken for fatherly were it not for cold, black fire in his eyes. He set the lamp on a rough-cut wooden table in the corner and slowly circled her chair, undressing her with his eyes.

"I apologize for the discomfort you must be in. My men tell me the restraints are necessary to protect you from yourself."

"Who are you, and what do you want with me?"

"I am Don Victor Carnicero, though that will be unimportant to you unless you please me. I sent for you, because you and your colleague have been searching for me. I am easily found by a beautiful woman." He stroked the underside of her chin with an unexpectedly tender finger.

"You won't get away with this. My colleague . . ."

He cut her off with a laugh. "Your colleague is a dead man. The timing and circumstances have only to be arranged. The same may well go for you, though I am prepared to give you a choice."

"What choice?"

"Please me." He tore the buttoned bodice to her dress, scattering little gray buttons across the stone floor like so many dried beans. He stepped back. Half lids draped his gaze. He nodded. "*Sí.* You might do nicely."

"You might die in your sleep."

The slap snapped her head back in a burn. "Such talk is unflattering. It can also be fatal. You are warned. Think of it. The next time you see me, we shall see if you please me." He picked up the lamp, stepped into the hall, and plunged the room back into darkness.

Cane stood watch at first light. Golden spears sliced across the mesa painting the *hacienda* adobe pink. The gates opened. A buckboard drawn by a long-striding mule pulled out, a single, serape-wrapped driver wearing a sombrero at the lines.

"Longstreet."

Beau threw off his blanket and scrambled through the rocks.

Cane lifted his chin. "What do you make of this?"

"Could be a supply run into town."

"Could be. Could be our way in, too. Saddle up and follow that jasper. I'll keep an eye on things here."

Minutes later Longstreet squeezed up a lope down the trail toward town.

Santa Fe

Longstreet jogged his horse up Palace, bright morning building to midday heat. The buckboard parked in front of a general store, the mule hip shot in his traces. He drew rein and stepped down a block south and across the street. There he could keep an eye on things without attracting attention. Without attracting attention at least until Trevane came striding across Lincoln from the government corral wearing an anxious expression.

"She's gone, Longstreet. Any idea where she is?"

"Who's gone?"

"Samantha. I didn't see her all day yesterday. When she didn't show up for breakfast I had the hotel check her room. The bed hadn't been slept in. I've looked all over town. I can't find a trace. I'm afraid something's happened to her."

"I'm afraid you could be right."

"What do you know?"

Longstreet glanced around. "This isn't a topic we should be discussing standing on a street corner."

"Then let's find someplace to talk."

"I can't at the moment. I think I know what happened to her. You'll just have to trust me for now. Get yourself a horse. We can talk on the way."

"On the way where?"

"Get yourself a horse."

Two hours later the supply laden buckboard pulled out of town headed for the *hacienda*. Longstreet and Trevane rode out minutes later.

"All right, out with it: what's happened to her?"

"It looks like *El Anillo* grabbed her."

"What makes you think that?"

"Cane and I think we've found the head of the snake. We've been watching a *hacienda* our ferret-faced friend operates from. Yesterday, he and three gunnies showed up with a female captive. They had a hood over her head, so we didn't recognize her. I had a gut hunch. Now it makes sense."

"They abducted someone, and you didn't try to help?"

"Oh, we'll try to help all right, but you're not going to just drop in on this place without an invitation or serious cover."

"So what do we do?"

"We start with that buckboard up yonder."

CHAPTER FORTY-THREE

Severio wheeled the buckboard around a curve in the trail. A masked rider, gun drawn, blocked the trail.

"Let me pass."

"I give the orders here."

"Fool. I serve Don Victor. Do you value your life so little?"

"I know who you serve. Now step down."

He made no move. The buckboard rocked as a second gunman climbed up behind him. Before the driver could turn in his seat a blow to the temple felled him senseless.

Trevane stepped down from his horse. Longstreet rolled the driver off the buckboard. They took his sombrero, serape, and peon pajamas. They tied him up in his long-handles and dragged him into the rocks along the roadside. Longstreet lifted his chin to the driver's clothing.

"Put those on and drive. I'll lead you to our next stop."

Orange and pink sunset sank into purple peaks in the west as Longstreet climbed the trial toward the mesa top followed by the buckboard trailing a spare horse. Cane climbed down from his perch at the mesa rim.

"What have we here?"

"A way into your box."

"What about him?"

Trevane pushed the sombrero brim off his face and grinned.

"What's he doin' here?"

"That captive the ferret brought in yesterday."

"Samantha," Cane said.

"Grab your gear. We'll let it get a little darker and then have Trevor take us on in."

Cane smiled. He collected his Henry rifle and saddlebags packed with fuse and four bundles of dynamite three sticks each. Longstreet removed enough supplies to hide him and Cane under a tarp in the cargo bed, while Trevane picketed the horses.

"How do you plan to play this?" Trevane said.

"Drive to the gate," Cane said. "They let you in, best we can tell there's a plaza inside the gate. The kitchen should be around toward the back of the *hacienda*. Exactly where is anybody's guess. Likely someone will show himself to help you unload. We'll have to subdue whoever that is. After that we head for the west wing of the house."

"Why the west wing?" Longstreet said.

"I've never seen a light on in that part of the house. Once we get inside, we'll just have to play it as it comes."

"How many people do you figure are in there?" Trevane said.

Cane clenched his jaw. "Good question. We know the ferret had three men with him when he abducted Samantha. Somebody opens the gate. Assuming *Señor El Anillo* is in there, at least six, likely more."

They exchanged eye contact in the gathering gloom.

"Let's get on with it," Cane said.

The buckboard crested the mesa. Trevane got his first look at the fortress estate. *Samantha . . .* she was in there somewhere. *We're coming.* Questions gnawed at him. *What kind of odds were they facing? What would they find? Would they find her in time?* And the sharpest realization of all—*it mattered.* He drew up to a dark archway in the pale adobe wall. Heavy wooden doors creaked on their hinges.

"You're late, Severio! Cook is furious."

Trevane ducked low under the brim of his sombrero and chucked the mule across the plaza angling east toward a low outbuilding set in the shadow of the back wall. A lighted doorway framed a heavyset man wearing an apron.

"What took you so long, imbecile? I had to prepare the Don's supper without all the desired ingredients. If he is displeased, it will be on your miserable head." He barely waited for the buckboard to stop before he lumbered forward to unload. He pulled back the tarp. A bright blade flashed in the low light of the door, the point resting against the fleshy underside of his unshaven chin.

"Make the slightest sound, and it will be your last," Cane hissed.

Trevane stepped up behind the startled cook and shoved a gun in his ribs.

"Inside." He followed the cook into the kitchen. He cracked the man's skull with his pistol butt. The man fell like a dressed side of beef. Trevane tied and gagged the man, dragged him into a storeroom, and blocked the door with a chair.

Back in the yard he climbed onto the buckboard seat and drove west into the shadows of the wall behind the *hacienda*. Cane and Longstreet climbed out from under the canvas tarp. Cane shouldered his saddlebags and led the way toward the west end of the hacienda.

She ached. She ached from the cold. She ached from the bindings. She ached from the unknown and frustration. Sitting on the rigid chair in the dark gave her little to contemplate but discomfort. Day and night had no meaning. A hulking brute came with food and a chamber pot at intervals she could not estimate. She tried to imagine Trevor. He would know she was gone. What would he do? She couldn't conjure up a way in which he might find her here. What did Carnicero want with her? Ransom? It seemed unlikely. "Please me," he'd said.

Boot heels clipped the tiles beyond the door. Keys jangled. The lock clicked. Lamplight stabbed the darkness. She blinked. The brute's frame filled the doorway. He set the lamp on the corner table along with a small bundle. He untied her feet and arms. She rubbed her wrists. He tossed her the bundle. A silken gown in a lovely apricot hue.

"Put this on. The Don wishes you. Knock when you are ready." He stepped out and closed the door.

Please me. That must be it. She shed her ruined dress, assessing the possibility of overcoming the brute. Even should she manage it, then what? How many others might she face? Better to take her chances with the old man. He might let his pleasure get in the way, giving her opportunity. She slipped on his gown.

The west wing of the *hacienda* was dark as it had been ever since they'd taken up watch. Cane inserted a blade and easily defeated the ancient latch. The door creaked open to a corridor dimly lit by a splash of starlight. He led the way inside, followed by Longstreet and Trevane. A row of shadowed doorways lined the corridor. Off to the left a stairway climbed to the second floor. Cane approached the nearest door and listened. Nothing. He drew his Colt and tried the latch. The door opened onto an empty chamber, lighted by a windowed door at the back of a darkened room. He crossed to the door, cracked it open, and peered into the yard at the back of the *hacienda*. He could make out the shadow of the buckboard where they'd parked it. Light glowed from the east wing and central halls above. He closed the door and returned to Longstreet and Trevane.

"This end is quiet. It doesn't appear there's a watch."

"What then?" Trevane said.

Longstreet looked up the stairwell and lifted his chin.
Cane nodded and led the way.

CHAPTER FORTY-FOUR

She tapped on the door, conscious of her skin by the light touch of silk. Now what? *"Please me."* She steeled her resolve.

The door swung open. The behemoth in need of a bath and a shave seemed not to notice her undressed condition. "This way."

He propelled her down a corridor toward a lighted stairway. He followed close enough for her to feel the heat of him. The narrow stone stairwell spilled out at the back of an expansive tiled foyer cut with corridors and archways. A grand stairway spiraled around a massive chandelier, disappearing in shadow on the floor above.

The goon pointed up with a cracked fingernail. Of course. Off to the right at the back of the house three of the Don's gunnies huddled around a small table playing cards over a bottle of tequila. Odds of wriggling out of this hole dwindled as she started up the broad staircase. The landing on the second floor branched off in hallways running in both directions. Light seeped under double doors at the head of the hall on the right. The goon gave her a shove toward the light. He opened the doors.

Hidden in the shadows of the darkened west wing, Trevane and Longstreet recognized Samantha instantly. Cane sized up her guard.

★ ★ ★ ★ ★

Don Victor stood in the parlor to his personal suite, impeccable in white linen. He smiled, appraising the drape of her gown tied with a sash. His eyes flashed approval.

"*Muy hermosa.* Very pretty indeed."

He might betray himself yet. She favored him with the hint of a smile as she took in the room. The hulk nudged her inside.

"Call if you require anything, *Patrón.*"

It was a warning. He closed the door.

"Please, have a seat." He gestured to an elegant settee drawn up before a massive fireplace, snapping and popping to the faint smell of mesquite. "Would you care for some sherry?"

She nodded, buying time to read the rest of the situation while he poured crystal glasses from a matching decanter. The parlor adjoined his sleeping chamber, with a massive four-poster bed visible in candlelight beyond a second set of double doors. Worse yet, no sign of anything that might be considered a weapon.

The Don presented her glass and took his seat beside her.

"You shall find my hospitality far more pleasant than my confinement." He lifted his glass.

"I'm sure I shall. Pity it took us so long to get to this point."

"I needed to be certain you would appreciate the delicacy of your situation. Now, may I offer you some nourishment before we . . . become better acquainted?" He twirled a tendril of her hair on a forefinger.

"You mean the food is better up here, too?"

He laughed. "Many things are better up here."

He turned to a sideboard laden with savory dishes and began preparing plates.

"I'm curious," Samantha said.

"You know what they say about curiosity and the cat."

"I doubt you'd find me pleasing as a dead cat."

"I should think not."

"Then indulge me."

"I plan to."

"Curiosity first."

He brought her a plate of warm tortillas and a thick chicken *mole*.

"Now, what is this curiosity that pesters you?"

"*El Anillo*. Do you own it?"

He fetched his own plate. "Own it? There is nothing to own. I am *El Anillo*. My word is the law of the ring. Nothing we seek escapes us. Even you." He took a bite of tortilla.

"So you were behind the diamond mine swindle."

He smiled. "It turned out that way. Most lucrative actually for a spoiled transaction."

"Spoiled?"

"It started out as a simple fence for a jewel thief. When he was unable to deliver the full value of his contract, he came up with the idea as a means to spare his life. It might have worked, too, if he'd been satisfied with his share. But, no, when he had the misfortune to lose his share, he wanted more from us. He wanted an escape for which he couldn't pay. I find greed an offensive sentiment. Don't you agree?"

"I'm afraid I must."

"Ah, *sí*, you are learning. Very nice. Now it is your turn."

"You have a curiosity?"

"No, no. Your turn to indulge me."

CHAPTER FORTY-FIVE

The big gunny lounged on guard at the door.

"Samantha's in there," Trevane whispered. "We've got to get her out."

"What do we do about him?" Longstreet nodded toward the guard.

"Give me the sombrero and serape."

Trevane handed over the clothing, taking Cane's hat and saddlebags in exchange. He hefted the bags to his shoulder.

"What the hell have you got in here?"

Cane smiled, donned the serape, pulled the sombrero's broad brim down over his eyes, bent his knees slightly to disguise his height, and started down the darkened corridor at a slow shuffle. The guard turned at the sound, reached for his gun, and paused.

"Severio, is that you?"

"*Sí.*" Cane shuffled closer.

"What are you doing up here?"

Cane pulled back the serape only slightly. A flick of the wrist buried a bone-handled blade in the big man's throat. His eyes rolled round and white with a soft, choking gurgle. Cane reached him in a stride, caught the body by his belt, and lowered it soundlessly to the floor. He waved Longstreet and Trevane down the hall.

"My turn." Trevane handed back Cane's hat and saddlebags. He donned the serape and sombrero, drew his gun, and motioned Cane and Longstreet to either side of the door. The door swung open.

Don Victor's demeanor snapped from amorous anticipation to black rage.

"Severio, what is the meaning of this?"

Trevane lifted the sombrero brim with a smile. A cocked pistol appeared from the serape folds. "Make a sound and you're a dead man, Don."

"Trevor," Samantha said, closing the sash to her gown.

"The very same. Looks like I'm just in time for the party."

"My men shall see who is dead. You'll never get out of here alive."

"For your sake, old man, they better let us pass peacefully. Beau, take care of the prisoner while I look after Samantha."

Longstreet stepped through the door gun in hand with a grin.

"Beau, you too?" Samantha said.

"And Briscoe. You've got enough knights here to start your own roundtable."

"Another fool," Don Victor said.

Longstreet leveled his gun. "Quiet, old man. Now let's get out of here."

Trevane took Samantha by the arm and led the way out of the suite and down the corridor to the west wing. The Don followed, Longstreet's gun at his back. Cane scratched a lucifer and lit a cheroot. He followed down the darkened corridor.

Footsteps sounded on the staircase behind them. Cane paused. Escobar crested the landing, nearly stumbling over the dead guard.

"Asesinato! A las armas!"

Boots sounded on the tiles below. Escobar dashed into the Don's suite. *"Patrón! Patrón!"* He raced back to the stairs. *"Patrón* is missing! Find him!"

Boots scattered below. Escobar dashed down the stairs.

Cane touched the tip of his cheroot to the fuse with a hissing flash. He watched the sizzle a moment, judging the burn. He pitched the bundle down the corridor and ran for the west-wing stairs.

The bundle bounced and rolled to the head of the stairs. The second-floor landing erupted in a ball of flame and smoke. The concussion shook the *hacienda,* raining a shower of marble chips and stone across the once-elegant entrance foyer. The blast threw Escobar to the floor narrowly clear of the crush caused by the central staircase collapse and the shower of crystal shards from the shattered chandelier overhead. He scrambled to his feet and ran to the *hacienda* plaza.

Trevane reached the buckboard. He helped Samantha up in the bed while Longstreet loaded the Don and covered him. Cane ran across the yard and climbed onto the buckboard seat beside Trevane.

"What the hell was that?" Trevane said.

"What was what?" Cane said.

"The explosion."

"Oh that. Bag's a little lighter. Let's get the hell out of here."

Trevane wheeled the buckboard back toward the kitchen and slapped lines to the mule. Almost at once muzzle flashes bloomed from the outbuilding shadows and east wall of the *hacienda.*

"Everybody down," Cane said. He slid off the seat. "Cover me and be ready to roll when I give the word." He slipped into the shadow of the compound wall and started toward the outbuildings.

Trevane lay down two rounds of covering fire.

"You best call off your dogs," Longstreet said. "It'd be a shame if you was to catch a stray bullet before the law has its way with you."

The Don hunkered down beside Samantha in the buckboard bed. "You're the one they're shooting at."

Longstreet added a round to Trevane's covering fire.

"Not exactly the indulgence you were expecting," Samantha said.

"Shut up! I will deal with you in due course in ways far more satisfying than simple pleasure."

"Tough talk for a man on his way to a long stretch in prison or a short stretch on a rope."

"Bold words for one still captive in my house."

Cane eased down the wall. Close enough. He pulled a bundle out of his bag, drew a blade, and cut the fuse short. His cheroot came aglow. He lit, threw, and flattened face down in one fluid motion. The bundle arced like a firefly toward the outbuilding wall. The wall disappeared in a thunderous flash, blowing up a storm cloud of adobe and dirt.

The mule reared in its traces. Trevane fought for control. Longstreet handed his pistol to Samantha.

"If he so much as farts, shoot the son-of-a-bitch."

"My pleasure." She leveled the gun.

Longstreet leaped from the buckboard bed to settle the mule.

Cane jumped to his feet. "Roll!" He trained his Colt on the darkness waiting for a muzzle flash to reveal a target. None came.

Longstreet threw his coat over the mule's eyes and led the frightened animal forward. He drew a halt for Cane to climb on, withdrew his coat, and rejoined Samantha in the back bed, relieving her of his gun.

Trevane clucked to the mule and wheeled around the east end of the hacienda. The gate appeared, a shrouded dark shadow in the wall across the moonlit plaza.

CHAPTER FORTY-SIX

Dust and debris from the outbuilding blast lay like a carpet across the plaza. Escobar sent two of his men to the west side of the *hacienda*. He and another took cover behind the well in the center of the plaza. He dispatched two more men to the gatehouse.

"Do not let them escape!"

The buckboard wheeled around the east end of the *hacienda* into a cross fire.

The mule buried its hooves, once more rearing in its traces.

Cane shouldered his Henry, turning his fire on the west end of the *hacienda*, buying cover. "Everyone into the house."

Trevane jumped down from the driver's seat and lit up the well; muzzle flashes pricked the night as he backed toward the *hacienda* doors. Samantha scrambled out of the buckboard bed and ran for the door. Longstreet shoved Don Victor off the bed and prodded him into the house. Cane and Trevane followed, backing and shooting.

A silvery wisp of moon lit the foyer inside, leaking from some fractured opening in the walls above. Cane handed Samantha his Forehand and Wadsworth.

"Keep an eye on him." He lifted his chin to the Don. "Trevane, cover that back west-wing corridor." He disappeared in the darkness as instructed. He handed Longstreet the Henry. "Beau, get low in the doorway and cover the west end, while I figure out what to do about the well."

Shooting fell silent.

"*Señor* Cane!" Escobar called. "Release *Patrón* and we will let you live."

"You would be wise to take such a bargain," Don Victor said. "It is more than I would have offered."

"And more than you'd keep the moment we let you go," Cane said. "Now, if I were you and valued my life, I'd call off your men now."

"And miss the opportunity to exact my revenge? What kind of fool do you take me for?"

"Revenge? In case you hadn't noticed, you're under arrest and on your way to trial for a long, long list of crimes. Maybe you hang and maybe you don't. It won't matter if you get gunned down here. Here's a promise, though: if we don't all make it out of here, neither will you."

"You speak as a man in control. To me, you and your arrest are a temporary setback. No more than an inconvenience."

"We'll see."

"*Sí*, we shall see."

"Speak to me, Cane!" Escobar called from the well.

"Call off your men and let us pass, or you and your *Patrón* will regret it."

Escobar smoothed his moustache in the web of his thumb and forefinger.

"Keep them covered." He dropped back to the shadow of the gatehouse. "If they try to make a break for it, shoot the mule."

Keeping to the shadow of the wall, Escobar eased his way west and down the wall to his men at the west side of the *hacienda*. "This way." He led them through the unlatched door to the west wing.

"I got company coming," Trevane said.

"Beau, give Trevane some help. I think I got the well figured out. Samantha, if our friend there so much as wiggles his inconvenient ass, shoot him."

Longstreet scrambled to the west-wing corridor. "What have you got?"

"Something let a little light into the far end of the hall."

"Must be the door we came in."

"What I figure."

"Any movement?"

"Nothing I can see."

"I got up top," Longstreet said.

"Up top?"

"The staircase is gone. The second floor ain't."

"Got it."

Longstreet eased away from Trevane's position to the cellar stairwell Samantha had exited from her cell earlier in the evening. With the stairway to the second floor blown away, it yielded a good view of the opening to the west-wing corridor above. He trained the Henry and waited.

Something scraped in the depths of the first-floor corridor. "Got movement over here," Trevane said and fired. Muzzle flash blinded the darkness; the report exploded in confined space. Two return shots blossomed. Trevane followed the first flash with a shot. A groan sounded. A body hit the floor.

Movement sounded up top. A shadow leaned over the shattered remains of the landing. Longstreet cut loose with the Henry. A body toppled over the edge, landing with a sickening smack on the staircase rubble.

"Two down," Trevane said. "At least one unaccounted for."

Hidden in the west-wing stairwell, Escobar held his breath. His mind raced. *What to do with both his men down?* He snatched a glance around the corner into the darkness. Nothing.

Cane studied the well in low light and the gate shadow beyond. *First things first.* He drew a bundle out of his saddlebag, measured the fuse, and cut it. He drew his cheroot to a glow, touched the tip to his fuse. Bright flared. A tiny comet broke the doorway shadow, trailing an orange tail as it arced over the well.

The blast threw dust, rock, and bodies into the air illuminated in a blinding ball of fire. Debris rained down on the plaza and the squeals of a frantic mule bucking in its traces as the concussion died away.

Trevane picked up a piece of stair railing. "Keep a sharp eye, Beau." He hissed and threw the wooden rail into the darkened corridor. It landed with a clatter.

Escobar fired into the darkness.

Trevane fired into the muzzle flash.

Escobar slumped to the stairs and lay still.

The gate stood quiet in the shadow of the wall. Cane looked for movement. He saw none. "Beau, what have you got back there?"

"Three down that we know of. Quiet now."

"Hold that position. Trevane, come back up here and help Samantha with our friend."

Trevane scuttled across the dark foyer floor to Samantha's side.

"Where do we stand here?"

"Cane took out the bad guys at the well. Looks like you and Beau got the action from the west end. That leaves the gate."

"Do you think they've got men there?" Trevane said.

"I would, wouldn't you?" Samantha said.

"Have to assume they do then."

"That's how we have to play it," Cane said.

"All right, Cane, we're all in place," Trevane said. "What do you want us to do?"

"I'm going to blow the gate. When I do, you take Samantha and the prisoner and get to the buckboard. Beau?"

"Yeah?"

"You got rear guard, but move fast."

"Don't need to ask twice."

"I'll rush the gatehouse just to make sure. Don't forget to pick me up on the way out."

Trevane smiled in the low light. "After all this? I'll try to remember."

Cane dropped to his belly and crawled across the plaza toward the ruins of the well. The gatehouse stood quiet. He estimated the throw. He'd be exposed to make it. He should have had Trevane cover him. Too late for that now. Surprise was all he had to work with. He pulled the last bundle from his saddlebag, measured the fuse, allowing time for throw and distance. *Got one chance to get this right.* He puffed his cheroot to light.

Trevane sighted glow. "On your feet."

The Don scowled. Trevane jerked him to his feet by the collar of his shirt.

"Get ready, Beau."

"I been ready all my life."

Samantha smiled to herself.

The fuse popped a bright sizzle. Cane rose and threw. Muzzle flashes blossomed in the gatehouse. Hot lead sliced Cane's shoulder as he dove back to cover. A fiery tail hit the ground, bounced once, and rolled to the foot of the gate shadow. The portal burst in a fireball, leaving an adobe dust cloud and smoke where a pair of stout gates once stood.

Cane broke from the well, zigzagging his way toward the gatehouse.

"Move!" Trevane shoved the Don toward the buckboard with Samantha in tow. Longstreet backed out of the *hacienda,* keeping the Henry trained on the second-floor corridor and an ear cocked to the first floor.

Someone groaned in the gatehouse. Cane flattened beside the door.

"Shoot the mule." Someone choked.

Cane fired twice through the open gatehouse door.

Samantha held the Don at gunpoint on the buckboard bed. Trevane climbed into the driver's seat as Longstreet scrambled onto the back of the bed, his gun trained on the *hacienda* door. Trevane slapped lines, and the mule kicked up a jog toward the gate. He checked the mule as Cane climbed onto the passenger seat. In an instant, the buckboard drove into the night, trailing a light cloud of dust silvered in pale moonlight.

CHAPTER FORTY-SEVEN

Capital Plaza Hotel
Santa Fe

Longstreet, Samantha, and Cane, his right shoulder bandaged and arm in a sling, sat in the elegant dining room enjoying steak dinners. Trevane stood watch over the Don at the jail. None of them trusted anyone or anything in Santa Fe to hold the prisoner. The sheriff seemed relieved to have his captors maintain control of their prisoner.

"So, what do we do when we get him to Denver?" Samantha said.

Cane lifted a brow over a forkful of steak. "We keep goin' to Cheyenne."

"You mean you don't think Denver can be trusted to hold him?"

"Didn't hold the ferret more'n a couple of days when we caught up to him a year ago," Longstreet said.

"But, if you cut the head off the snake, don't you think it will die?"

"It might," Cane said. "Then again it might grow a new one."

Samantha dabbed her lips and took a swallow of burgundy. "Seems like a lot of trouble for a job that may be finished."

"Just bein' cautious," Longstreet said.

Cane fished his pocket watch out, fumbling it open with his unpracticed left hand. "I suspect Trevane must be gettin' hungry 'bout now. I'll go on over to the jail and spell him."

"You sure you're up to it?" Longstreet said.

"Even left handed, I can handle that old man."

"There's pie for dessert," Samantha said.

"Have a piece for me." He pushed back his chair.

"I'll relieve you around midnight," Longstreet said.

"You'd only wake me. They got a spare cell with a bunk. Just be on the morning stage to Denver."

"Suit yourself."

"You, too." Cane headed for the door.

"I think he just gave us his blessing." Samantha half-lidded her smile.

Beau filled her glass and topped up his own. "What about Trevane?"

"Sweet boy. I like him—sort of like an amusing puppy; but he's no Beau Longstreet."

"Kind of you to say."

"I know of what I speak. Does your widow?"

"Not exactly."

"Pity to let all that go to waste. You owe it to yourself to figure things out, Beau. You only go around once you know."

"I s'pose I do."

"But not until you do, is that it?"

He smiled. "She vexes me."

"Vex is a funny way to admit you're in love."

"Takes two."

"My point exactly."

He covered her hand with his.

"Am I interrupting something?" Trevane said a little frosty.

Longstreet shook his head. "I was just taking leave."

"Sit down, Trevor," Samantha said. "I'll have another glass of wine while you wrap yourself around some supper."

"You two have a pleasant evening," Longstreet said and wandered out into the night.

Denver

Longstreet threaded his way through lengthening shadows up the tree-lined street toward home. *Home.* He fought the feeling of estrangement that never failed to haunt him after these long separations. He'd made their report to the Colonel, while Cane accompanied Samantha and the prisoner to Cheyenne. Trevane tagged along, hangdog at the prospect of Samantha returning to Chicago. They didn't need him. Cane told him to go home; Samantha agreed. So here he was opening the gate and turning up the walk. He climbed the porch and considered a knock. *"You owe it to yourself,"* she'd said. He opened the door and stepped into the polished foyer.

She appeared in the kitchen doorway. "Beau! You're home."

"I am."

She crossed the dining room, wiping her hands on her apron. "Miss me?"

"You don't miss a beat do you?"

"You said you'd consider it."

"I did, didn't I?"

"And did you?"

"I may have. Some."

"Considered some?"

"Missed some."

"Be still my heart."

"Sit down in the kitchen and tell me about your adventures while I finish preparing supper. Richard is away so we will be joined by Abigale."

The story spilled over to the supper table with a catch-up summary for Mrs. Fitzwalter. Longstreet noted Maddie pricked attentive to every mention of Samantha. By dessert, she served apple pie secure in the knowledge Samantha was on her way back to Chicago.

"Fascinating," Abigale said. "Mr. Cane's use of dynamite

must have been terrifying."

"Only if you were on the receiving end."

"I don't know how you do it, but, fortunately for the law abiding among us, you do. Now, if you will excuse me, I'll retire to my room. I'm sure you young folk have some catching up to do."

She said it with a twinkle in her eye. Beau rose and held her chair. They watched her go before beginning to clear the table.

"You don't have to help with that, you know. You've only just returned home."

"I have returned home."

She glanced over her shoulder as he followed her into the kitchen with a stack of dirty dishes. Maddie washed. Beau dried. Finished, she peeled off her apron, hung it on a hook, and smoothed her dress.

"Would you care for a glass of sherry?" Beau asked.

She shook her head. "The good Irish stuff."

"Sure an' begorrah, a lass after me own heart." He mocked her accent.

"You are insufferably persistent."

"I warned you."

She went to the sideboard and poured two crystal glasses. She led the way to the parlor. She scratched a match, lit the lamp, trimmed the wick, and took a place on the settee.

He slid in beside her, accepting his glass.

She lifted hers. "Welcome home."

He touched the rim of her glass. "Good to be home."

They took swallows.

"So how much?" he said.

"How much what?"

"You said you missed me some. How much is some?"

"That depends."

"How can that 'depend'? Either you did or you didn't."

"Samantha must have been very grateful. By my count you saved her life at least twice during your little adventure in Santa Fe."

"Oh, that. If you must know, she's still of the opinion we're both fools."

"Good."

"Good?"

"If we're both fools, that means I'm not alone in my foolishness." A little mist appeared in her eye. "In that case, I confess. I did miss you."

He took her in his arms. She lifted her lips and welcomed him home.

"Comfortable?" she said.

"I am."

"So am I. Come along." She rose and took his hand.

"Where are we going?"

"I'm going to show you a closet."

CHAPTER FORTY-EIGHT

San Quentin
One Year Later
Warden Johnson sat in the haloed light of his desk lamp. He blew across the rim of a steaming cup of coffee and took a small swallow. He opened the coroner's report on his desk and read.

Jeremiah Endicott, prisoner 13467, found unresponsive in his cell 7 September 1879. Attempts at revival failed. Cause of death poison of undetermined origin. Third finger, left hand severed. Whereabouts unknown.

Johnson closed the report. *El Anillo.* He'd seen it before. Quick, clean, untraceable, unmistakable retribution for those who needed reminding of The Ring's power. Endicott was in for fraud. A mining scheme, as he recalled. High-profile investors in San Francisco had been bilked out of serious money. New York, too, as he recalled newspaper reports of a sensational trial. They'd recovered some twenty cents on the dollar. Endicott became a fall guy for the scheme. They'd arrested one Don Victor Carnicero, who was charged with being mastermind of the diamond mine swindle. Pinkerton testimony claimed him to be head of *El Anillo,* but that couldn't be proven. They had enough on him to put him away for ten years. Endicott's demise made it clear—*El Anillo* was plainly still in business.

The guard paused at an oversized cell at the end of the block. He plied a ring of keys for the one to open this door.

"You have a visitor, Don Victor."

Rested and relaxed, the Don closed his book, set it on a side table, and rose from a stuffed chair. He was clad in his customary white linen in stark contrast to the coarse, striped pajamas worn by the occupants of other cells. His double cell was comfortably furnished and stocked with cigars, tequila, and amenities generally withheld from other inmates. Anything could be had for a price, even in prison. The guard followed him down the block to a staircase and then down the stairs to the visitors' room. He unlocked the door. The Don entered with a smile.

Escobar rose. *"Patrón."* He bowed.

Don Victor took his seat at the visitor table across from his man.

The guard left them to their privacy, locking the door in his only concession to regulation. Little of the Don's incarceration could be considered regulation.

"How are my appeals progressing?"

"The lawyers are working on them."

"Tell them to work faster. I am rotting in here."

"Sí, Patrón."

"And my assets?"

"Your liquid assets are secure. I was able to remove them from the *hacienda* the night you were taken."

"Bueno. We will not be able to return to the *hacienda* now that it is known. You must find a new location we can occupy once I shake the dust of this pig pen from my feet."

"Are they not treating you well, *Patrón?* The bribes have all been paid. If they are taking the money and not living up to the bargain, we can make an example of them."

"I know that. We are not being cheated. It is only the confinement. I grow impatient. This is a temporary setback. Temporary needs to end."

"*Sí, Patrón.*"

"The geologist?"

"As you wished, *Patrón.*"

He smiled. "*Bueno.*"

"Is there anymore we can do?"

"Oh, there will be blood one day, my son. There will be blood; but I must be there to enjoy it."

"*Sí, Patrón.*"

Mexico

A warm, gentle sea breeze rustled a curtain of palm fronds, securing the privacy of the low, walled patio. The sun filled the horizon with a fiery red ball, painting running ridges of cloud pink and purple. Fading light rested warm on his face. Bright spears of red spread across the caps of blue Pacific waters. The Counselor sipped a tall, cool drink, mellow at the end of the day. His days passed in idyll here on the plaza to a comfortable adobe on the grounds of an elegant hotel property. A modest monthly fee availed him of all the hotel's services in his own home. A remarkable find for the comforts provided. He paid little heed to news north of the border, though one couldn't help hear reports of the fall of the once powerful Don Victor Carnicero. He'd been fortunate to disappear when he did. Others had not been so fortunate. Endicott had been tried and convicted. He read newspaper accounts of the trial. His part was mentioned in passing, though no one could identify him beyond his alias. He smiled. Poor Endicott hadn't lasted long in prison. They may have imprisoned the Don, but even that could not put him out of business.

In the end, he'd outsmarted them all. A simple cutout. He'd

disappeared without a trace. Lost in this tiny coastal community, known to only a few of the very rich. He'd become an anonymous denizen among a den of the anonymous and discreet.

Approaching sandals slapped the tiles. He glanced up as a dark-complexioned waiter in a starched white coat set a drink on the table beside him.

"I did not order this."

The waiter smiled. "Compliments of an investor."

Investor? He bunched his brows. His mind raced.

Gould!

Spanish steel entered his brain behind the right ear.

Searing cold. Burnt black.

Eyes fixed the horizon.

Sandals padded away on the tiles.

Shady Grove

Another story had come to an end. His head nodded. I let him have the moment, ruffling the pages of my notes to put a fine point on all I'd just heard. He snorted awake.

"Sorry, Robert. I might have dozed off there for a moment."

"No trouble. Gave me time to put these messy notes in order. We were on a breakneck pace there at the end. I wanted to make sure I'd taken it all in. So, Counselor escaped the league, Pinkerton, and *El Anillo* only to be found by Gould. Remarkable. Did you ever find out how he managed that?"

He shook his shaggy mane. "Never did. I suppose if you've got enough time, money, and determination, you can find out most anything sooner or later."

"The law's promises of protection didn't do Endicott much good."

"Nobody's perfect. Endicott set himself up when he threw in with Carnicero in the first place."

He coughed some, deep in his chest. I waited until it passed.

"And the Don's appeal . . . was it successful?"

"Not right off, but that's another story."

We lapsed into silence for a time.

"Then it appears we've come to the end of this one."

"I believe we have. As it's turned out, we set out to teach you what we learned about precious stones. Now that you are an investor, it seems you've surpassed us."

He said it with a conspiratorial wink.

"I shouldn't think so, Colonel. I learn new lessons here each week."

"Thank you for that, son. Time passes, and so do I."

I sensed our time for today at an end.

"Is your bottle secure?"

He nodded and nodded off.

CHAPTER FORTY-NINE

Shady Grove

I arrived at Shady Grove that Saturday with only a few lingering questions to complete my notes on this most extraordinary story. Somber struck me the moment I entered reception. The nurse in reception, to whom I had become a familiar visitor, cast her eyes down upon seeing me. Penny met me at the door to the solarium with tears in her eyes.

"He's gone."

"Gone?"

"Passed in the night. Oh, Robert, I'm so sorry."

She hugged me. I held her. It mattered not we were in her place of employment. *The Colonel was gone.* Realization hit like a slow-moving freight one was unable to escape. The man who brought us together. The irascible old curmudgeon who'd turned me into a whiskey smuggler was gone. He'd called me *son*. I wept.

We stood there for some time, hugging and weeping. At last I managed some composure.

"May I see him?"

"They've taken him to the undertaker."

"What of funeral arrangements?"

"He has no known next of kin."

"I'll make them. Did he have a religious preference?"

She shrugged.

"I'll take care of that, too, then."

247

"Oh, Robert, it's so good of you to do this."

"He called me son. It's the least I owe him. That and a proper obituary."

Material for the obituary was at my fingertips in the archives of the *Denver Tribune*. I was able to reconstruct the Colonel's many contributions to law enforcement and ridding the west of all manner of miscreants, scoundrels, and outlawry. Stories abounded. Stories I told and others that might never be told for the loss of my beloved narrator.

Beloved. Yes, I admit it. I'd grown to love the crotchety old character. I respected him from the first time I met him. For that, I took his abuse, though I came to understand most often his teasing was full tongue in cheek. I think Penny came to love him, too, in spite of his incessant complaining. In some ways he was central to our relationship. We revolved around my weekly visits with him and his vicarious involvement in everything we did. He was either with us or close by always. And now he was gone.

I made funeral arrangements at Holy Redeemer Episcopal Church. We'd no idea what his religious preference might be, but I reckoned all of us could use a little redeeming. That and the fact the lovely little church was not far from Shady Grove with a similar mountain view. I hoped he'd feel at home there, with no concern for what he might be fed for lunch.

Internment was arranged at Good Samaritan Cemetery near the church, once again with a good mountain view. Good Samaritan seemed appropriate, too. As an officer of the law, he certainly qualified. He'd rescued me from feet of clay for the love of my life. And now in death, I suppose, I returned the service in some small measure.

The *Denver Tribune* was more than gracious in publishing the Colonel's obituary and announcement of his arrangements.

They treated his passing as a front-page news story in light of his considerable contributions to settling and taming the territory. The story earned me my first front page byline. Even in death it seemed he looked after me. I wept again.

Legendary Rocky Mountain Crime Fighter Passes

Colonel David J. Crook, US Army (retired), passed away peacefully this week at Shady Grove Rest Home and Convalescent Center in Denver. Colonel Crook is credited with having organized and directed the legendary crime fighting association known as the Great Western Detective League. The Colonel and his network of law enforcement professionals operated across the West for more than two decades in the latter years of the last century to rid the territory of all manner of lawlessness and criminality. The genius of Colonel Crook's Great Western Detective League transcended the limits of law enforcement jurisdiction, promoting cooperation among peace officers through the exchange of information. Colonel Crook turned the telegraph and railroads into crime solving tools as they worked in tireless pursuit of preserving law and order. Born March 30, 1825, in Chicago, Illinois, to Horace and Emily (McHugh) Crook, Colonel Crook served the Union Army of the Missouri with distinction throughout the war of secession. He moved to Denver following the war and soon took up his career in law enforcement, serving two terms as Arapaho county sheriff. Colonel Crook will be memorialized Saturday morning in funeral services at Holy Redeemer Episcopal Church, Denver, with internment to follow at Good Samaritan Cemetery.

The day of the funeral dawned sunny and cool. A day the Colonel might have indulged a blanket to warm his legs and hide his bottle. I smiled, patting the bulge in my jacket pocket. Penny accompanied me to the church. She'd been a great help with the arrangements. She'd also observed the church would make a lovely setting for a wedding. That, too, seemed appropriate. Present in spirit, he'd approve.

The church infused a sepia glow with scents of furniture polish and candle wax. Attendance was sparse as one might expect for one so old, mostly staff from Shady Grove and a delegation from the Denver police constabulary, attending out of respect for the man's many contributions to modern day law enforcement. As we entered the church and walked up the aisle we passed one unfamiliar figure tucked quietly away in a back corner of the last pew. Penny and I took places at the front near the coffin and bowed our heads.

Father Taylor conducted a thoughtful service in spite of not knowing any more of the Colonel's history than what he could learn from Penny and me. He invoked the Archangel Gabriel in adding a spiritual quality to the Colonel's career dedicated to law enforcement for the good of all. By the time he drew the service to a close, even those who scarcely knew the Colonel must have held him in high regard. I suspected he would be a trifle embarrassed by all the flowery accolades but not altogether displeased at the recognition and remembrance.

Pall bearers, hired for the occasion by the funeral director, loaded the casket into the hearse for the short journey to the cemetery. The polished black hearse with glass sides was drawn by a handsome pair of high-stepping, black carriage horses. Penny and I fell in behind along with the smattering of mourners who made their way to the cemetery. I noted the man from the back of the church, bringing up the rear of the procession. Something about him tugged at the back of my mind, though in the press of matters at hand I put those thoughts aside.

At graveside, Father Taylor commended his spirit to the Lord's care, inviting us all to bid our personal farewells. And then it was over. The crowd began to drift away in silence or subdued conversation. My Penny was engaged by one of her coworkers so that I found myself standing there with the man wearing a duster and worn Stetson. There was something familiar about him, though I was certain I'd never seen him before in my life. Hickory-hard frame of angular construction, features stitched in worn saddle leather. I ventured a speculation.

"Mr. Cane?"

He lifted a watery eye below his hat brim. "Do I know you?"

"No, sir. But I know you."

"What can you possibly know of an old reprobate like me?"

The words came to me unbidden as a voice from the past.

"I know, for example, you favor a pair of fine-balanced, bone-handled blades, one sheathed behind that .44 holster rig and the other in your left boot. I know you can draw and throw with either hand fast enough to silently defeat another man's gun draw."

He arched a brow.

"I know you are equally fast with that Colt and a .41 caliber Forehand & Wadsworth Bull Dog rigged for cross draw at your back. Some consider a spur trigger pocket pistol the weapon of choice for a whore. Such a notion would sadly misestimate your use of it. Those that do, seldom do so for long."

His eyes narrowed in a squint. "Last time I heard that palaver it was him talkin'." He lifted his chin to the grave. "That where you got all that, Mr. . . . uhh?"

"Brentwood, sir. Robert Brentwood. As a matter of fact, it is. I'm a writer, you see. I've written books about your exploits in the Great Western Detective League."

"Heard something about that. Not much of a reader myself, other than Scripture."

"Would you possibly have time for lunch with my fiancée and me? I'd like to get to know the man behind my stories."

"Young feller, at my age all I got is time."

"Splendid! Let's be on our way then . . . Oh wait. I almost forgot." I drew the whiskey bottle out of my coat pocket and reached over the graveside.

"Hold on there just a minute, young fella. That looks like a perfectly servable bottle of Old Crow."

"It is and a longstanding secret we shared."

"How so?"

I glanced over my shoulder and lowered my voice. "I compensated him with a bottle each week for telling me his stories. They didn't permit liquor in the rest home."

"You smuggled it to him?"

"I did."

He laughed. "You're all right, Robert Brentwood. I would like to get to know you, too. Now before you do anything as rash as to have that bottle buried with him, hand it over. I've got a story or two I can tell, and Lord knows he has no further need of it."

I glanced from bottle to grave and quickly concluded the Colonel would approve if the stories were to continue. I handed him the bottle.

"Do you suppose we could share a dram with him for old times' sake?"

He glanced at the bottle and handed it back to me. "You do the honors, son."

Son. I took it, blinking a little mist from somewhere, pulled the cork and poured a couple fingers worth on the casket lid. I corked the bottle and handed it back to him.

"Now put that in your pocket. My fiancée was his nurse. Even she doesn't know of our little arrangement." We started for the gate where Penny waited. "Do you live in the area?"

"Got a room over on Aspen. House used to belong to the Widow O'Rourke."

"Maddie."

He lifted a brow. "The same."

"Whatever happened to Mr. Longstreet?"

"Long story. Come by for a visit. We'll talk."

I smiled and waved at Penny. "Look who I've found."

AUTHOR'S NOTE

This story is loosely based on an actual mining swindle that took place in the early 1870s. Wealthy investors from San Francisco and New York were successfully defrauded by hucksters who salted a mine field with precious stones in Colorado. As is true of this series, the Great Western Detective League is also loosely based on Colonel David J. Cook's Rocky Mountain Detective Association, which did in fact operate across the West in the latter decades of the nineteenth century. Past the bare facts of the case, the author has created a fictional story for the entertainment of the reader.

ABOUT THE AUTHOR

Paul Colt's critically acclaimed historical fiction crackles with authenticity. His analytical insight, investigative research, and genuine horse sense bring history to life. His characters walk off the pages of history into the reader's imagination in a style that blends Jeff Shaara's historical dramatizations with Robert B. Parker's gritty dialogue.

Paul's first book, *Grasshoppers in Summer*, received finalist recognition in the Western Writers of America 2009 Spur Awards. *Boots and Saddles: A Call to Glory* received the Marilyn Brown Novel Award, presented by Utah Valley University.

Major library review magazines consistently praise Colt's "lively writing style, fast action, complicated plots, and flashes of humor."

To learn more visit Facebook @paulcoltauthor.

The employees of Five Star Publishing hope you have enjoyed this book.

Our Five Star novels explore little-known chapters from America's history, stories told from unique perspectives that will entertain a broad range of readers.

Other Five Star books are available at your local library, bookstore, all major book distributors, and directly from Five Star/Gale.

Connect with Five Star Publishing

Visit us on Facebook:
  https://www.facebook.com/FiveStarCengage

Email:
  FiveStar@cengage.com

For information about titles and placing orders:
  (800) 223-1244
  gale.orders@cengage.com

To share your comments, write to us:
  Five Star Publishing
  Attn: Publisher
  10 Water St., Suite 310
  Waterville, ME 04901